ZOMBIE00

BRAD GOOCH

THE OVERLOOK PRESS

WOODSTOCK & NEW YORK

First published in the United States in 2000 by
The Overlook Press, Peter Mayer Publishers, Inc.
Lewis Hollow Road
Woodstock, NY 12498
www.overlookpress.com

Library of Congress Cataloging-in-Publication Data

Gooch, Brad.
ZombieOO / Brad Gooch.
p. cm.
1. Zombies—Fiction. 2. Pennsylvania—Fiction. I. Title
PS3557.O478 Z44 2000   813'.54—dc21   00-026885

Book design and type formatting by Bernard Schleifer
Manufactured in the United States of America
FIRST EDITION
1 3 5 7 9 8 6 4 2
ISBN 1-58567-043-X

Chapter 1
How Zombie passed his earliest years in Truckstown, Pa.

I T ALL STARTED at the Everhart Museum. The way to the museum was blocked by a huge ugly fountain. What's the big difference between a sculpture and a fountain? The art museum was near a coal museum, where you descended into a cavern that was brightly lit. It was a wormhole. A fake coal mine. There was another mine a few miles away where they'd turn out the lights and you'd be lowered in a bucket to worship the cool blackness. I mean tour it, not worship it.

Anyway. There I was with my folks. They were nearby, in front or lagging behind. They were in their own world, I always thought. Now I realize it was I who was in my own world. The museum rose before us in a park called Nay Aug Park that never seemed quite right. The museum seemed quite right. It was made of tan stones.

The inside, though, is where the point is. The best part of the art museum was that it didn't have much art. Instead it had artifacts. I was often scared in there. I was scared by the gigantic black-marble-

and-onyx stairs. I was scared because there was no air. I was scared because of the feeling of ancient spells being released inadvertently. I knew none of the paintings on the walls had anything scary in them. So I tried the more adventurous and three-dimensional shows.

My favorite show was the glowing rocks, which you entered through heavy black drapes that hung down over the doorway. Heavy, weighted, leaden, black velvet drapes. You pushed your way in. Inside what seemed the smallest room in the world, a closet of a room, a horizontal case ran alongside the wall, low enough to view. Then there would be a trick with the lights. Either the electric lights of the chamber would be flicked off, or there never was any electric light in the chamber and the lights that would go snap would be those in the case, leaving only a phosphorescent glow of different rocks with veins made of blue chips of stars or of the green hair of moss. That's how magical it was, I swear. Then you'd leave with the rest of the onlookers. Not feeling alienated from anybody at all. The rocks cured me. They healed me. I really felt I needed to be healed.

I tried to carry that sensation into the rest of my life. I did it by growing moon rocks in my bedroom. You brought them to life by dropping a liquid chemical from an eyedropper held up in the air. The rocks slowly began to grow and ooze with pink and orange colors. So the transformation brought them into the same area in my mind as the glowing rocks at the museum. But those in the museum were geological and were protected.

The mummy produced in me a feeling similar to that produced by the glowing rocks. Of course none of these things mean anything to you. Glowing rocks? A mummy? Inside a room on the second floor was a mummy. The mummy was lying in a coffin or boat or shadow shaped like the silhouette about it, the way cartoon monsters are given dark or bright auras that hug them. It was wrapped in bandages. I was amazed that Scranton, Pennsylvania, was important enough to be entrusted with one of the ancient Egyptian dead. That made me feel a little better about myself, since Truckstown was located near Scranton.

But nothing compared to the sacred voodoo chamber. There the movies played in my head no matter what time of day or night. It was as if I were born there. Except when particles of dust were revealed dancing away by overhead schoolroomish lights and windows. I longed to be inside the sacred voodoo chamber. It barely looked sacred to anyone else, probably. Most of it was old, gray, grainy photographs taken by anthropologists and ethnopharmacologists. One showed a dancer pierced by needles. A colored one was a photograph of a woman in red. But late in the afternoon the oozing green candles they allowed to burn for dramatic effect picked up a glow from the crossed, burnished bronze weaponry. A round straw fan was tucked into a wall as well. I can't explain it. No one was there. The candles started talking to me. They talked without words, as in a dream. One said, *Look up to heaven!* I felt very special. To actually get a little bit of help and guidance from beyond.

That's when I knelt on the cold stone floor, which was swirling with veins of white and black coloring. My little legs were trembling. My knees hurt from the unusual pressure on them. I folded my hands together in a gesture of prayer and supplication. I was begging and saying thank you. My heart felt very warm for the first time in years. I was heating up my own heart. Or the forces were heating up my own heart for me. I inhaled rapturously.

Suddenly a stupid, fumbling hand was on my shoulder. The hand of an old fainthearted guard. I imagined he would be punished for this insurrection by the forces in the room. If not now, later. He was followed by my folks. They knew I wasn't hurt. They knew I was into one of my "acts," as they mistakenly labeled them. But they were mortified that this time the incident was taking place in public, not just within the entrails of our house. It showed them up badly. It said that something was wrong with them, not just with me. Which they knew too well, though it was never discussed in any way.

They rushed me out of there. Stashed me in the back of a car. Their car. Their lime green mobile, a stuck-together assemblage of metal and fur. We went

home without a word. Which is the way the proce-
dure usually went. What could they say to me that
they wouldn't really be saying to themselves? It was
a grisly way for a freak like myself to live. Especially
now that I had been made a zombie for the first time
in my life that I was conscious and fully aware of.
I'm sure there were earlier slips and slides.

The zombification often started with just such a
falling to the knees.

Chapter 2
What Mark and Zombie did at school.

MARK WAS THE first boy to recognize the zombie in me. His mastery had obviously been honed and perfected through centuries of practice. Even if he was only fifteen at the time. Or appeared to be fifteen.

I was on my knees in a field with scratchy grass and scents of spring. Across the street rose the weirdly royal sweep of the football stadium of wire fencing and bleachers and loudspeakers and the colored lights of flashing bulbs. I stared intently into Mark's scuffed bucks. Their thick rubber soles were colored deepest pink. He stood above me like a statue of himself. We talked in such a curious way that afternoon, the sun beating onto my bare back. I had folded my cotton shirt and was using it as a pillow to support my forehead pressed to the ground. I heard his words falling as if from the nearby trees hung with caterpillar nests. I was totally spaced. So, apparently, was he. Needless to say, we weren't on anything. They didn't have anything back there, back then.

"Come to my apartment. I have some movies I want to show you."

He lived in an apartment rather than a house, with his single mother.

"Why do you want to show me movies?"

"You have a lot to learn about the world on the other side of your mind."

"I love you."

"Don't even try it."

I had discovered part of the proof that I was becoming zombified was that I would just blurt out really wild, flowery, embarrassing things like "I love you." It was a kind of swoon I went into that would come out of my mouth. I later found out that zombies were known as the living dead. I wondered how that description of me, of us, stacked up against the very florid feeling and talking that went on, and still does, among us. I wondered if the dead felt more about life than the living.

That afternoon I went to Mark's for the first time. We watched eight-millimeter movies while lying on his bed. His mom was a peroxide blonde who looked like a white-trash tramp: pink pedal pushers, the whole extravaganza. I felt sure she had boyfriends who stopped by to molest her in the middle of the night. For instance, in the bathroom Mark's *Playboy* magazines were piled up. What kind of a mother would let her fifteen-year-old son put *Playboy* magazines on the top of the commode? A commode top covered with a shaggy pink rug?

I can't tell you how suffocating his bedroom

was. The floors were carpeted in brown shag. All
spaces were filled with model monsters, model boats,
model human bodies. He owned Werewolf, this
big muscular man covered in brown horsehair. He
owned a green Frankenstein. He owned all these
objects. Objects have a lot to do with turning a
switch in me on or off, depending how you look at
it. The bed we were lying on was covered in a dark
woolen blanket. I didn't want to get out. But I also
felt I wouldn't know how to get out if I wanted to. I
left that up to Mark, who was flooding me with his
collection of creepy crawly movies revealed in the
moonlit floodlight of a noisy projector behind us on
the ledge over the back of the bed. I'm tired of going
over and over them in my mind. The Lady Godiva
nude on her horse riding through a German town.
One man peeped out his shudder. I mean shutter. And
the usual zoo of monstrous men with foreign accents
lunging at me. I wondered if it was all some kind of
World War II propaganda. Mark never raised the
shades in his room. I don't even know if there was an
outside there, or an airwell, or a wall. So it was either
harsh electric light or dreamy projected light.

I worshiped him in either light. Because of my
nature, I don't have the usual friendships or loves.
Mark is the perfect example. When I was lying next
to him I felt a great light emanating from him. I saw
him as a wizard. I hung on his every word. I wanted
to walk through fire for him. I wanted to be hanged

for him from a high scaffold in front of lots of school kids. The psychology was very basic, very binary. It was all about proving that I was under his power, as if he didn't know already.

Which doesn't mean that I didn't have an accurate sense of Mark even without the nuances. His blond hair was cut unevenly short. He wore glasses. He belonged to no club. He had no friends. He dressed in khaki pants and button-down shirts. His voice was low for our age. I would love to know where he is today and just follow him around for a day.

That's what I did in those days. But there was nowhere to follow him but around his bedroom and into his mind. He would give me access to his mind whenever it suited him. Whenever we were talking he was giving me access to his mind. Otherwise we didn't talk. He decided when the talking was going to take place. It was heaven. I was completely relaxed. Whose hands was I in, after all? I was in the hands of the gods. At least the gods in what I would discover to be my religion, a very ancient and integrative religion. A religion followed by a number of invisible men and women. *We're all around you every day. But of course we would never be noticed. We're hiding in plain sight!*

"Fetch my ring, Zombie."

I forget how he started calling me that. It just fit. I loved the name's round twang. Its zany kinship with a song I'd once heard about purple people eaters and with the one-eyed monsters I'd seen in a movie about the angry red planet, Mars. When he called me that name I heard a soft buzz and the inside of my head went all blue. I associate that blue, blurry, buzzing sensation with love. First love.

I fetched his ring. The ring was a cheap plastic blue ring with gold plastic wings and stars on its perimeter. It came from a circus. Genus: "Merlin ring." I would slip it on his pale, crooked, freckled bent finger, then kiss the top of his hand.

"How did you get this way?"

"I don't know." I giggled.

"I want to take you to school."

"I don't even remember ever seeing you at school, Mark."

"That's because I'm in the high school building and you're in the junior high school building."

"Oh."

"What kind of grades do you get?"

"All A's."

"Amaaaazing."

I felt in that word a sarcasm that slashed and salved at the same time. The word as he said it was a put-down. He was smirking at me with his boyishly pink lips. Yet there was in his insistence a caring, almost certainly a closeness, as he wound his way into my insides.

"You free to go to my school tomorrow?"

"You mean just not show up at mine?"

"Yes. It will be as if you never were. That's a line from a curse. Gnya-ha-ha. From the Three Stooges."

"Yes. I will," I said as quietly as if I were taking a vow.

"Gnya-ha-ha," he repeated, making fun of his own maniacal manner.

I met Mark the following morning at the corner. He didn't speak to me but turned on his heel like a Prussian soldier and headed down the street toward school. The junior high school and the senior high school faced each other from opposite sides of the street. My heart was beating fiercely because I was used to being a good boy, an obedient boy, a boy who received all A's. I was of course still following my tendency toward obedience. But this time a lower, stronger power was doing the directing.

"I'm your puppet," I whispered from a half step behind.

"No you're not," he corrected. "You're my shadow."

I did pass that day feeling like Mark's shadow. Whenever possible he ignored my existence entirely. He hung up his jacket in his locker without giving me leeway to hang up my own cranberry-colored windbreaker, which I continued to wear throughout the day. Sometimes, when a teacher asked for an explanation, he'd call me his friend he had to watch for the day. End of discussion. Then he'd point to whichever wooden desk he wanted me to crumple into.

The tip-off was that he kept handing me his books to carry. Big, colorful bricks of geography, math, chemistry, literature. In art class he dispatched me to a pencil sharpener that glistened at the front of the room to insert his lead pencils for sharpening. It was like a buzz saw slicing logs of lumber. Sometimes I'd sit in front of him and he'd kick the back of my seat. That happened in a German class while the teacher was telling of her summer vacation in Bavaria. Sometimes I'd sit behind him and he'd pass me notes with words: "stepenfetchit," "aardvark." Those came my way in *David Copperfield* class.

All day long I felt as if my entire body were blushing. Especially walking down the halls. The high school was a very acute place. Everyone registered each nuance even if they didn't react or couldn't quite say its significance yet. I knew all those eyes were homing in on me. The screening of *Lady Godiva* had been good preparation for my day clacking along the tiled hallways filled with light from a central court-yard. It was a light and airy prison. But mostly I was stuck in my cranberry windbreaker, staring at my brown penny loafers. I didn't understand how I got this way. But I knew that the heat rising through my body making the pole of my spine as hot as a thermometer in a flu meant that I was in the right condition.

The only relief was a trip to the men's lavatory. All kinds of misfits were gathered there. I could relax. No one even noticed when Mark flicked his cigarette ashes in my mouth. The hoodlums stood peering in the mirrors, combing their slicked hairs, their combs acquiring a film of goo. I saw them from a great distance, as if they were in a movie. They apparently saw me that way, too.

They'd go in the stalls of the "lav," as it was called, to light up their rosy cigarettes, sending clouds of smoke into the rest of the white-tiled cell. All the smoke settled in my lungs, mixed with the breezes wafting under a partly opened frosted window from the airwell. We were bottom feeders. We fed on light and smoke and air. Then we were expelled by someone who came to the door in a weaselly suit.

"It's the end of the school day. Now comes the hard part."

"What do you mean?"

We were walking down the monumental front steps of the high school, where all the kids from across the street could identify me as not having been in class that day.

"We need to get you hurt. If you don't do everything I say, say everything I say, then it's all over and I just walk away, never to let you darken my door again."

"Why do I need to get hurt?"

"You need to realize your nature. It's the opposite of mine. You're from the reverse kingdom. You have opposite needs and responses. You're nurtured by pain. It's your black sunshine."

"Not pain pain."

"Pain pain."

Something about his matter-of-fact tone caused me to believe him.

Then Earl crossed our path. I didn't know Earl that well. He was short. He sometimes wore his hair cut in a Mohawk. He was on the wrestling team. But mostly he was one of those monsters who blocked my way home. He used to hang on street corners just to harass littler boys like myself. We had a history. Once he pushed me into the snow. Once he locked me in a basement with a burning coal stove, then threw rocks through the windows. How was that ever explained? Weren't my folks alarmed? Apparently not. I have no memory of any particular reaction, except my mother coming to fetch me from the back porch of the woman across the street who rescued me from the playful criminals. "What are you boys doing?" Why was that anomalous event so passed over? Or hushed up? Or was I simply and not so surprisingly zoned out while it was taking place?

Here was that same Earl, prowling. Mark let me know in unspoken language, like the way people talk in dreams, that I would soon be saying something to Earl to inflame him. And that the machinery of punishment would begin to turn and whir and recoil and lunge. I understood his excitement. It was matched by pure fear and regret on my side. I didn't want my precious head broken open.

I said the words. Something like "Your mother wears combat boots."

That silly bit of fluff became the combination to an important lock: not a silly lock at all. The words ground against each other, creating the force and momentum to open the safe filled with his emotions kept well under wraps in daily life in our small town. But they were definitely there, all dark and throbbing. Earl was their doorway, the octagonal doorway through whom blasts of lightness and contrasting darkness banged steadily.

Earl called to other boys. Since then I've heard this sort of whistle calling when prowling gangs call to one another in the night. Pretty soon they are engaged in a battle of baseball bats with the owner of a grocery store. I knew that I was the blood orange ripe for letting. I was the bait. I was "it." Of course I was made to be "it." Born, seemingly, to be "it." Happily destined in some conflicted, adolescent way to be "it."

I don't remember the words. There's no point pretending. I don't remember the actions leading into the wordlessness, either. But I remember the moat. It was the next of my big important spots marked with an X forever in my head. They made me go down into the moat, which ran alongside the basement classrooms of the high school building. I recognized the manila window shades from *David Copperfield* class hanging at half-mast as I stumbled down. There were no janitors inside to help me. No lingering teachers. The regular school kids had made their escape. Only the fringe element was left. It was our time of day. We were caught in the chink of escape between day, belonging to school, and night, belonging to family. *Am I completely crazy? Or wasn't it exactly like that? Does anyone else have such memories? Other zombies do. If there are any zombies out there, would you please get in touch with me? My name is printed on the cover of this book.*

Earl started punching me. He stayed away from my face at first. But he grabbed me by the arm, leaving a raspberry bruise. He punched me hard in the chest. He punched me in my back where my kidneys are. He kneed me in the balls. Then his friends came around. "Put him down, put him down," they chanted as I was slid down this moat with my hands dragging along its concrete wall. The drop was about three of my heights. They devised a rope for themselves for lowering into the pit. It was still broad daylight. Earl grinned at his handiwork from the railing above but did not participate.

Now it was just three or four of them and me. "What did you call Earl?" they'd say occasionally as a weak excuse for their session of torture. I was slammed really badly in the head by the back of a hand until I heard ringing. I tried to escape by smashing my head backward, only to rupture the glass window of a classroom. My head was briefly encircled in a halo of shattered glass that pricked my skin and sprayed me with blood drops. I was spat on. I was kicked. I was flung against intransigent walls. I was mocked. They called me names. They took my clothes away with them, having stripped me.

The last I remember I was lying in smashed glory on the pavement at the bottom of the moat. The perpetrators had departed, practically singing with the energy they'd siphoned from working me over. Blood was everywhere. I remembered a wounded robin I'd once nursed. I was nude and blood spattered and bruised with the stains of this embarrassing violence. I was simply embarrassed to be me.

Up above in a square of diminishing light was a window of brightness in which Mark was framed. He appeared luminous. He was only a teenager, but his badly marked skin had erupted, his hair turned to gold. His eyes were blazing. I squinted at him through a thin veneer of blood caked over my eyes. Those sweet hazel eyes of mine! Those broken eyes! I ran further and further into myself. Mark was visibly pleased. And then he was gone. Disappeared. Forever. Most of my masters are like that. Most of my friends, too. Is it me? No, it's something about zombiehood that unsettles people. But attracts a few weirdos as well, I must admit.

I fell asleep in an impossible position. It was as if I were drugged. When I awoke, every kind of imaginable pain set in. My body was aching as if filled with a black cloud of dust and gas that just kept becoming bigger and bigger. I wanted to cry. I couldn't cry. I felt that the flecks of blood all over my chest and legs were my tears. Men in tan uniforms flashed lights in my face. My body was exposed in all its paleness to relentless scrutiny by their flashlights. I heard the siren of a train chugging by on a trestle a few blocks away and imagined it was moaning and wailing for me. The birds might as well have fallen backward from the trees, I was feeling so sorry for myself, so horrified and repentant and just plain sick. I've dreamed of that spot many times since.

It wouldn't stop. The wretched out-of-control-ness. I found identification of the situation difficult. But when they told me they were taking me back to my parents, I knew from where the revulsion and self-doubt had arisen. It was my parents. They were wrong for me. They were simply humans, mortals. I was something else. All of these bruises and blood-stains were external. They were superficial wounds. But in their primitive recognition and satisfaction of a need in me, those boys had fulfilled an ancient sac-rifice. The only true hurt could come from my par-ents by their misunderstanding of my every move, word, and thought.

I returned home that night. Or rather I was returned home. There was a predictable scene of screams and lies. I made up some story. Nobody believed me, but they all wanted to go to sleep, the cops included, so they pretended to believe me. What else could they do? Investigate?

After I went to bed, my dad shuffled into the darkness as softly as a shadow. He was a short man, wound pretty tightly. But he seemed to have caught a glimmer of who I was and what was transpiring. I lay back in my Queen Anne bed with its four walnut posts that was left to me by my maternal grandmother in her will. I could make out my father's flannel robe, his glasses glistening in owlish outline. I knew he must be wearing the purple leather slippers with white fur lining he favored. I knew everything in the dark room by heart. Map of the United States. "Colonial" desk. Photograph of a mummy. Sewing needle taped to the wall that I imagined to be a Haitian syringe of temporary death. Only the moon rocks were visible, almost breathing with acidic purpleness and orangeness, like algae coming monstrously to life. Like the rocks of the moon that came to life and began grunting in a Saturday matinee movie my father and I attended while my mother was at sewing class in Scranton. Where the museum was. To me the moon rocks were the pulsing heart of my love for my stiff father.

"You're living in a different world," he said to me quietly, standing by my bedside.

"Yes, yes, that's it." I answered excitedly. I love it when somebody tells the truth. It's the one kind of talking that doesn't take any thinking at all.

"Maybe it's time you just moved into the garage, he continued evenly.

Wow! What an idea! It was time to leave home. Earlier than expected. I wouldn't have to wait out the general adolescent schedule until high school graduation for a polite excuse to split.

"Just don't bring shame on the family name," he pleaded, hushed but pleading nevertheless. "No scandals. Keep it as quiet as you can."

"Yes, yes, yes, yes, yes."

Moms usually garner praise for sensing the real deal with their sons. Yet so do certain fathers with certain sons. Often those certain fathers appear to have been the most distant, the most combative, the least communicative, the biggest assholes.

I imagined that night that my father must include some zombie in him, too, tucked away in his own DNA code, just a glimmer, a few small letters he'd managed to bury fathoms deep. He worked as a certified public accountant and adhered rigorously to the external uniform of most humans. He was very busy at income tax time. Genetics was the only explanation I could come up with for his remarks on that crucial night when I first tasted my own spilt blood, licking it off my fingers.

Chapter 3
The dream sequence.

WHEN I WAS SIX I was in the hospital for tonsillitis. I thought I was going to die from horror. From the shades on the windows. From the pain when my folks left me there. It was the first time I'd been away from home. And I wasn't a zombie yet. I love me there. That little boy in the pale white bed as if he were lying in a tomb of cotton and linen and light.

I had my own private room rather than a double room or a bed in a ward. Reason was that I was so frightened all the time. Not by solitude. By the other people. I would scream as loudly and fiercely as I could because I knew I could control the doctors that way. They were afraid my stitches would pop. I was controlling them through my remarkable ability to suffer extreme doses of my own pain. So my father bribed me by offering me a hundred pennies to take my shots. His deal was that the room was costing too much per diem. He was a certified public accountant, so he wanted to spirit me out of there to cheaper freedom. They wouldn't let me go if I wouldn't let them inoculate me with this medicinal glue meant to shut me up, keep me mollified. I took the bribe. The needle was shot into my tender behind. We went home, a happy family.

Since then I've had this dream every few years. The dream takes place in that hospital room on one of the nights I was left by myself. Now. I don't remember any of this ever happening. Of course. That's the only thing that bothers me about the dream. Otherwise it's simply phantasmagoric.

I'm lying alone in the hospital room. Boys are calling to each other nasty things they're threatening to do to each other. I smell the rosebushes through the window. Who should appear in the room but a man in a white lab coat? He has a tall bald dome of a head. He has the most beautiful light blue eyes that register in the near darkness as a kind of astonishment. Most striking is his height. Probably six feet four inches. I'm perfectly calm. Not like when I had bad dreams because I was scared the monster from the angry red planet was in the windowscape. Or that there were rattlesnakes snickering at the bottom of my bed.

Here's the action: he draws out a long silver syringe. Like a magnified yet more glamorous version of the ones I was so terrified of. He draws it out with a flourish, as if it were a sword in a medieval story of knights and black bats. He begins to fill its thinness with stars, a glistening powder of stars. Very much like the veins of the rocks I later saw again at the Everhart Museum. Blue and white bits of stars. Then he taps a black powder into its thinness. Black bits of clouds passing swiftly in the night. A trail left by the carriage of death. He takes my arm. He pats it lightly. He finds a vein. He injects the silky medicine within.

Here's how I felt: I felt a molten calm passing through me. I felt my veins and arteries turning into rivulets of death and dying. My blood turned. My reflexes diminished to nearly zero. Just the state a zombie master truly wants to enjoy. The light bulb in my head was lowered as if by a dimmer. Few vital life signs left. Then he walks out again, dragging his scythe behind him.

The important part is what he said. And of course that is the part that didn't exactly happen or that I don't exactly remember. Sometimes in the dream I do hear him speaking, I think. But usually I just know that he's speaking, and understand what he's saying. There might as well be music playing in the background for all the good his words do. But since I can understand him, although I understand him differently in different years, then I can translate a sense for you.

This is what he said: "I am injecting you with a potion of anesthesia similar to the dot of poison in certain puffer fish that can kill or can give the greatest joy. I know what I'm doing. So your odds are nine to one. Now you understand that by injecting you with death, I'm giving you an immunity to death, at least early death and natural aging. I'm inoculating you—to use a metaphor of a less advanced medical science. Conversations kill. So I won't go on too long. You'll live longer and more fully by showing fewer and fewer life signs. Believe me.

I could hardly contain myself. But I didn't need to because I was completely toxic from the potion of powder he'd instilled in my veins.

Chapter 4
Zombie's adventures in the garage and the funeral home.

L IFE IN THE garage was exquisite. It was a double garage. On one side, an old black Buick belonging to my thin paternal grandfather. The rest of the space belonged to me. A crappy mattress buckled lightly on the floor. A coal-burning stove. A tattered beach chair fashioned from green and white plastic crisscrosses. Oil slicks glimmered here and there. Windows paled over with exhaust fumes let in daylight as if it were cigarette smoke. When I was feeling down, I'd stretch my body by hanging from the rusted, netless metal circle of a basketball hoop hooked on the exterior of my secluded cottage.

A full-length mirror was tacked on one wall. I'd found it in the alley behind the garages of the other houses. We didn't live in a particularly rich neighborhood. In the mirror I discovered I barely made an impression. It was apparently part of my nature that no matter what I wore I would appear as a nerdish nonentity. My extremely short hair was stuck severely to my head. A little dab of hair glue made no difference. I wore my white shirt with top button buttoned, green cuffed pants, and black tied shoes. I blew on my hands to annihilate the germs I imagined nesting there. No matter what combinations I tried, I always achieved this zero degree of impression. Standing on any street corner, I was indistinguishable from anyone else. Without personality. Like an ignored homeless person on the street asking for money. I saw all that forecast for myself already in the magic mirror.

My haircut had a lot to do with that. And of course that haircut could be traced to the barbershop where I first fell in with a bad crowd. Here's how it happened. My father gave me an allowance of $2.50 every week. My favorite way to spend it was to allow the barber to shear my hair on Thursday afternoons after school. (I had perfect attendance except for the one day I already described when I was beat up.) The barbershop was located across the street from something called the American Auto Store. This was a fabulous store filled with rubber tires, wastebaskets, artificial lawns. Outside the barbershop was attached one of those old-fashioned tubes of blood wrapped in bandages.

I didn't love the shop simply because of the haircuts or because of the mirrors in which I disappeared. I loved it mostly because of a pile of smudged, worn comic books stacked on a side table of chrome and spackled white plastic. That's where I first became drawn to stories about boys with flattops and girls with pigtails. Soon enough I graduated to fiercer comics filled with violence and perversity and bloody colors. In one a sheer force of darkness inhabited a spiderweb. In others superheroes were forced to deal with their cosmic lives by struggling with the inarticulate limits of speech balloons. I adored one comic book in which a ripping, clawing critter plunged his hand into a zone of blue ozone to excoriate victims whose red sinews were revealed in all their tautness to the illustrated page like stripped carcasses of beef swaying in a butcher shop of pain.

The noise was driving me nuts the day Mitch walked in. The noise, that is, of the shears. The barber was an interesting guy. Joe. He used to hunt down all the hairs of his customers in a most pleasing, candyass way. He seemed more like a thirtyish male Florence Nightingale than anything else. His ruddy Irish face was round and pure and smiley. His voice was soft and polite and somehow cultivated or something I couldn't understand that was at odds with his gray workshirt and buckled knuckles. He was like a manly man with a woman lodged somewhere in him. I'd probably do better with understanding what was attractive, and unusual, about him if I saw him today.

These types would barge in and put Joe to the test in front of his customers. Mitch was one of them. That's when I began to worship Mitch. Paulette wasn't with him yet, the first time. I began to worship her later, as part of a couple. This is how it happened. I was seated in the barber's chair. Mitch ambled in menacingly. With him, Walt Creek. And a tall, lithe young man with a tattoo of a freakish woman on his forearm. They put the barber to the flame somehow. I felt they had some hold on him, as if they were blackmailing him. It was as if he were in a tight spot. But that he enjoyed the tight spot, too. I couldn't figure it out. It doesn't matter. It was merely the occasion for Mitch to realize quickly and instinctively that I could be had. That I was a zombie.

I'd love to tell you about Mitch and his discovery of my true nature. (Nothing thrills me more than having someone discover my true nature without being told.) He and his friends were circling about Joe. Mitch was smiling as if they were friends. It was as if Joe were one of them, ran with their pack. But I knew that kind of snarly smile. It was the smile Mark had smiled when he pretended to be impressed that I got all A's. It was a snarly, wolfish smile. They were all circling around each other in a tangled, swirling helix of domination and submission, aggression and self-protection. I could practically taste the danger. It tasted like my own blood.

"You feel like going out to the lake with us?" Mitch asked him.

"No, I'd rather not," Joe answered.

"You might well have to," Mitch answered.

Luckily for all of us, Joe was saved because Mitch finally caught my image in his eye, like an irritating speck. When he saw me, I saw him. Really saw him. And saw Joe, too, in the same fashion. I mean, I saw that Mitch was quite tall, that his hair was shaved to near baldness, obviously a prison haircut, and that he spoke flatly, always with a clique around him to praise and laugh and egg him on. He wore pointed black ankle boots with ridges in them. He wore black jeans. His shirt was inconsequential, something you'd buy at a factory outlet.

I saw that he was a voodoo master used to having zombies at his beck and call. I saw in X-ray fashion—as Superman could see through the walls of buildings—a black tail, like a whip, that flared in the center of his body. I saw fire that singed and burned and hurt badly. It was the kind of fire they'd stuck people's arms into in the past to make them recant. That's when Joe's doubleness of posture made sense. He wasn't just a barber. He was a witch doctor. He may even have called Mitch there that day to possess me, to drag me off in his teeth like a cat a rat.

"What you looking at?" Mitch asked me.

No one had ever talked to me with such authority before. I felt a melting sensation. What was melting? The false exterior of myself that accompanied me at most times publicly through all those childish years.

"I was looking at you, if I might," I answered, not knowing from where came the strength of voice to actually speak.

"I thought so."

Just writing down the words as they were spoken

doesn't help much in conveying the story. I mean, we could have talked about a TV show and it would have amounted to the same thing.

Either way the words were that moment's ful-fillment of an ancient curse.

"I like to steal," Mitch really did say. "You interested in helping me?"

"Yes," I squealed. I was so happy. My heart was burning in my chest.

"Then get out of that chair and take a walk."

"Totally."

I was lowered into the backseat of the jalopy they drove around in. Walt Creek was driving. Mitch sat in the suicide seat. Next to me was the morose one who didn't speak much. We were the silent back-seaters. They were into crime, those boys. They were bad boys. I became the perpetrator of much of the bad stuff. I was the stool pigeon, the patsy, as well as the executor of the most defiant gestures the rest were too protective of the limits of their skins to carry out. Mitch thought it all up.

So this is what I did. I walked myself into a dark lake, inky black and dark and cool, submerging myself entirely in this baptism while they laughed and hooted and clapped. I felt so good stepping out covered in wet muck. It was a satisfying performance. A revelation of who I was. A baptism. I longed so for that kind of surrender. Then I held up a hardware store, holding a gun in my hand that was unconvincingly heavy, truly a dead weight. I swiped three hot dogs from a roadside stand without paying, without turning around to acknowledge the screams. All this was taking place on roadways that curved out of sight of Truckstown into black forests and long, meandering valley roads. For me it was truly a joy ride.

Weirdly enough, I never got caught. They got caught. It was the benefit of my inability to make an impression, of my invisibility. Whenever I was with Mitch, my heart rate lowered to about half, breathing to less than half, blood pressure so low I needed to slump back in my seat to preserve my own consciousness. When I walked into that hardware store in broad daylight I felt nothing but peace and quiet. It was like walking through the calm before a storm. They gave me the money from the cash register and the safe. But when they came to tell the police, they could only describe the other boys. Of course the authorities didn't do anything. These were teenagers in a town that knew little crime. So they gave them a haircut and sent them home. I remember vividly the day Walt Creek reappeared in civics class with his scalped head, from prison. Everyone must have been in awe of him. I certainly was. He gave me a look that pretended to say, "You got off, you dirty cheat," but that really said, "This is our bond, this is what proves our friendship." I knew he didn't mean it. But I loved him there nevertheless. Walt's place in my heart, though, was always usurped by Mitch when he reappeared.

"Lick my arm," Mitch said the first time he saw me after his light prison sentence.

Our reunion took place in front of the impressive stairs leading up to the senior high school. Mitch was challenging the very pillars and carved stone eagles by taking the expanse of those stairs as his own private command center, beginning each day after four in the afternoon. That was the time of day I've already described when the teaching authorities and janitors disappeared. I realized early on that these were false authorities, cardboard authorities. Mitch was the real thing.

"I want you to meet my new girlfriend."

The hidden sweetness of that remark, and its absolute rightness, impressed me greatly at the time. I wanted nothing more than to meet her. She was the Paulette I mentioned earlier.

"Let's pick her up from Bible class."

"Okay." Then I added in an afterthought, which was totally a non sequitur, "I like to steal, too."

The ride to the church was uneventful. Along the way Mitch related to me what he called the facts of life. These consisted mostly of a lot of biological facts about what men and women did together to make babies and to have fun. I'd actually read it all before in a vermilion medical book I'd found once on my parents' bookshelf. He talked about radical changes in his body that rang true to my own experience: hairs growing as thickly as dark grasses, juices flowing, voices changing. I never found those changes to lead to any of the biological practices he described. I had no inclinations in that direction. But I was realizing that my consciousness of my zombiehood, the growth of the strength and power of my own powerlessness, had exactly paralleled the efflorescence of those symptoms, of that coming of the season of spring to the body. That's why when I'd been admitted to the hospital with tonsillitis many years earlier, I could say that I hadn't truly yet become a zombie. This slow process culminated at puberty.

Screeeech.

We pulled up in front of the Methodist church with a loud roar. Mitch made a fuss with the car. Its motor was grumbling and recharging. He honked. The church was a colonial number with a white New England steeple: all white clapboard and red brick and clear windows, not stained. Paulette stepped out. She had been incarcerated in the annex of the building, where the classes took place. Her Bible study wasn't driven by any inner peace. It was a punishment imposed by her parents. But she used it as a cover to get away. Her girlfriends covered her by saying they had gone out afterward for pizzas or French fries with mustard. All the kids were unhinging from their families at different speeds, along different trajectories. Mitch and I were the only ones unencumbered. Mitch terrorized his mom. He didn't have a dad. And he terrorized his two younger brothers. So he continued to live in his house in a bad neighborhood. Mine was the freedom of total exile and banishment.

When I saw Paulette for the first time I couldn't believe my eyes. Yes. She was beautiful. But more than that she was feisty, she had lots of attitude. I saw her immediately in terms of the biological changes Mitch had just described. She stacked up quite well against his description of the female animal entering into the heat of puberty. Her breasts revealed themselves alertly, pertly, through the thin pink material of a cotton shirt. Her dyed hair was lemony. She was wearing a very short green-and-red skirt of plaid material: the design seemingly borrowed from a package of Scotch tape. Her legs were healthy, muscular, curved. They made me think of horses leaping. Paulette's shoes were cordovan penny loafers that clapped onto the pavement. A few folks waiting for their free bag lunches at the ledge of a window at the church gave her dirty, winsome looks.

When she slammed herself into the car, she and Mitch stuck their tongues down each other's mouths. Then we drove off abruptly.

"That's Zombie," Mitch introduced me brusquely.

He was using the nickname that had begun to stick. When I graduated, my space in the yearbook was marked by a black square. I'd never visited the portrait photographer to have my picture taken. Who'd remember me, anyway? I had never participated in any class activities except that I ranked high on the honor roll because of my unvarying A average. (In that sense I'd modeled myself on Mark. I wanted to keep it clean.) The only information they had on me was my nickname they printed under the black square: "Zombie."

Mitch and Paulette liked riding the wind, breaking things and people. Or at least imagining they were. "I want to spoil you," Mitch said to her once. She cracked him in the side of the head for that one as she reached down to activate the cigarette lighter installed in the dashboard. I leaned forward, waiting for her to remove it from its boiling cylinder, just to see its orange eye of fire. I imagined that Paulette had just such an orange, fiery eye between her legs. Mitch liked to poke her there with his middle finger. Sometimes she'd bury her head in his lap as he was driving as if she were a fanged white poodle. It was sweet.

We committed the usual crimes: holding up drugstores, holding up gas stations, holding up nickel-and-dime operations, candy stores, and the like. I did most of the wielding of the gun. But as I explained earlier, I never got caught. Mitch did. Paulette did. Pretty soon they were both bounced out of school, and Paulette out of her family. She simply moved in with Mitch. They'd "sleep it off," as they called their sound slumbering every day until four or five. Which gave me the opportunity to fulfill my perfect attendance record at school. In spite of my grades and attendance, though, I was never elected to the Honor Society. The authorities just couldn't bring themselves to that brink of amorality, knowing as much of the situation as they did. Which was fine with me. It would have destroyed my equally flawless presentation in the yearbook. Or maybe I just wasn't honor society material. I'm not sure. But Mitch was becoming increasingly angry. He recurrently felt the heat, faced the clink. It was against his code of honor to rat on me, even if they stuck his arm in the fire. Which they didn't . But he did hold the matter against me. Eventually his salivating for revenge and for punishment of my entirely passive infraction had consequences.

"Get me a drink, Zombie?" Paulette asked in her inimitably hard and soft manner. She was chewing several sticks of gum at the time.

On one of the nights I remember most fondly, we were all three lounging in the family room of Mitch's house. "Family room" meant basement. He had taken up residence there. He'd scavenged a couch bed. A TV. A circular, padded red bar with full bottles of liquor lined on a shelf behind. The dartboard on the wall was a center of attention. Paulette loved to let darts fly as if they were arrows and she a warlike goddess. That night they kept me busy with chores. I ran to the corner to buy the pizza pie. I ran upstairs for pepper. I painted Paulette's toenails orange. I found the channel on the TV. I wish I could remember what movie, or filmed play, we watched on the educational channel. All was in black and white.

I knew this fantastic chance for nearly being one of them couldn't last. Eventually Mitch and Paulette turned away. They left me in the dust. I heard Mitch say something, mutter something. "Precious sweet, don't make me weep." Wow! All that from a criminal. Mitch could speak in the most beautiful and unusual ways. What did Paulette say in response? As I remember, she said, "Did you ever think of having two girl-friends at once?" Needless to say, there was no room for me. I curled up in front of the TV.

Soon enough my neck was on the block. Don't make me go on. "*Go on!*" Mitch sold me down the river. I guess it's what I wanted. What we wanted. He knew that I couldn't be caught under normal criminal conditions. So he devised a plan. I walked into the funeral home with my arms extended. They were sitting in the car parked out front on Main Street, daring me to do so. I mean directing me to do so. Making the warm, gooey chip in my brain glow an amber orange.

I held a silver revolver in my light, fragile, shaking hand.

When I walked into the funeral home with my arms stretched in front of me, they were laughing their behinds off. I went into the front parlor room. It was about seven-thirty at night in the wintertime. Who'd ever think to latch the front door of a funeral home? Expecially one that looked like a plantation house brightly lit on the most traveled boulevard in town. It was a magnificent place. I made a sharp right.

My instructions were to stand in the center of the front viewing room and raise my gun to each and every light fixture in the ceiling or in freestanding lamps and blow them out with dangerously aimed shots. I did. But I hadn't counted on the presence of the preserved corpse of a man, dressed like a banker, his hair slicked back like a vampire's, his pancake white face set in a bemused expression perhaps meant to convey contentment. He watched the whole thing. I watched him watching me. It was one matter to be observed, caught, handcuffed, accused by humans. They seemed to be on the other side of a barrier of sight, feeling, and sound. But he was right there. In the same distorted zone as me.

I wished I had Vaseline to spread on his face and hands. To give some perspiration to the presentation, some sweat, some glistening conviction. But I didn't. So I just shot away to his even enjoyment. I loved all the finery in which he lay: the purple satiny lining to his box, the lacy frills about the pillow beneath his head, the pale Swedish wood in which he was encased. A curtain of scary darkness fell. For a sweet, still moment it was just me and him.

Soon all chaos broke loose. There was a lot of screaming. A woman, horrified, broke into the darkness. Pretty soon a man with a flashlight appeared fast behind her. Alarms were sprung. Dogs barked at the top of their form. I just waited it out. I knew the machinery of the trap was now beginning to grab me in its metallic contraption. The policemen came.

Mitch had planned this brilliantly. Only with no get-away and my body as evidence would they ever remember to capture me. Capture me they did. They took me disdainfully, disinterestedly, to our small-town jailhouse. There wasn't even a cell. I was made to sit in a long hallway. Just me and the posters tacked on bulletin boards. The clock clicked in the next room. Luckily I was still a minor.

All that remained was to slip down the other side of an inevitable hill. The agent of the action in this case was again my father, condensed as he was into a fury of embarrassment. This was the very kind of infraction he had forbidden me. He stood now in a wash of green light from the bulbs in the hallway ceiling. A deal's a deal. My only regret was that I wouldn't be able to say good-bye to Mitch and Paulette. I had seen their stupefied, grinning faces in the windshield as I was led to the police car, its bloody beacon swirling. Rain was falling. That was good-bye. Farewell. Adieu.

I won't even tell you what my father was wearing or looking like in that hallway. The pain of looking at him was too much. In my bedroom we had transacted our business in the dark. In that sickly, green, glaring public light he felt the pressure to take a more exaggerated, strained view of things.

"When your grandfather died he left three hundred dollars in an account for you that he'd scrimped and saved all his life for. Here it is. Now get on the next bus out of town."

Arrrrrgh. That was it. I didn't feel the same exultation this time. I felt truly bad. That was the next to the last time I saw my father and the last time I saw Truckstown ever again. The only fully rounded memories I have of him are three: giving me the hundred pennies to take a shot in my behind in the hospital when I was six; giving me leave to live in the garage; kicking me out of town with a small inheritance.

At dawn I was ensconced at the Greyhound station. The next bus was in an hour. I had no bags, just my shirt and shoes and baggy pants and my hands stuck into their bottomless pockets. The boarding of the bus was mechanical, desultory. About an hour into the trip through the cavity of the Delaware Water Gap with the sun rising over its ragged cliffs, I turned to the fat woman on the far side of the aisle who was knitting her granddaughter a cap, as she'd told everyone within hearing three times now.

"Where's this bus going, anyway?" I asked.

"New York. Where did you think? The heavenly city of Jerusalem?"

She let out such laughter and disbelieving howls that the driver had to interrupt on the intercom to ask everyone to remain calm. I was on my way. Or on the way that had been prescribed for me.

Chapter 5
How Zombie made his way
in the big city.

NEW YORK CITY scared and dazzled me that first
morning so many years ago. I felt dizzy much of
the time. I walked through the midtown area near the
Port Authority Bus Terminal where I'd disembarked.
Frightened of heights, I hugged the buildings. I thought
I was going to fall. It was one of the stronger frights
I'd ever sustained. I knew this was the place for me.
A place where I could live in constant terror and
anonymity and challenge. I sensed that there were lots
of zombies all about me. I saw others holding on to the
edges of buildings for dear life. But no one seemed even
to see them as they scurried by on business. This landscape was a welcome mat to a lost soul such as myself.
It was as if the noise of the city were a gigantic rock
band, speeded up, revving, the volume made unbear-
able. Everyone's minds had obviously been tampered
with by the mere repetition of the drone. They had all
been worn to a nub, some more than others, as I had
been worn down naturally within my own hometown
in a different manner.

I ran my hands over my face, trying to sponge up the cold sweat as I stood at a street corner, unable to cross, afraid that I'd be swallowed in a river of traffic. If anyone ever needed a true zombie master or mistress, it was me right then and there. I feared that the cars would eat me up and suck me into their technological bellies without anyone ever hearing a bang or a whimper. I had long ago begun to exhibit the symptoms of neurogenic shock: cold sweaty skin, weak irregular pulse, irregular breathing, dry mouth, dilated pupils, reduced flow of urine. The difference was that my shock syndrome had apparently been instigated by a dream. *The Dream!*

I walked and walked the entire day until my very skeleton ached with the feeling of having been abandoned, left to wander the earth like the Cain I'd heard so much about at the Methodist church. I loved going to church. I loved going to school. I loved serving Mitch and Paulette. Now whatever was I going to do? The architecture became less threatening as I stumbled downtown, the buildings lower. They snuggled bending streets and avenues more believably. They were no longer fierce deities needing to be worshiped yet disdaining all offers.

On a pewter lamppost I found a pasted sticker for a club. The drawing showed a zonked guy with his arms held out in front of him as mine had been during *The Great Funeral Home Heist!* His eyes were glazed with solar systems. Underneath they'd labeled him

"Zombie." Oh my God. It was my high school yearbook all over again. A giant wedge of destiny had squeezed into my teeny, uncomprehending mind. What else could it be? The club was called the Little Prison of the Château de Sade. I didn't know what that meant, so I ripped down the flyer to have the vitals and waited until it was night before I started in its direction, asking my way at every street corner. The white and pistachio lights of oncoming cars and lampposts were forbidding.

Finally, night. I had been waiting, waiting, waiting. Killing time. As the night shade thickened, more people on the streets seemed to be my first cousins, their attitudes as beaten down and inexpressible as my own. I asked this one. I asked that one. Finally I neared the approach to the club, its sign matching that of the flyer I clutched in my quivering fist. I really felt abandoned. Hot tears were coursing down my vague face. I was filled with the pain of the ages. Nothing is worse, even for a zombie, than to go unrecognized for such a long stretch. Even the dead need *some* reinforcement.

The man at the door laughed. "You've got 'sucker' written all over your forehead," he remarked inexplicably. Then he pointed my way down an incline of stairs as steep as a rope ladder, almost as precipitously vertical as the descent into Mark's moat when I was in junior high. At the door they asked for scads of cash. I handed over nearly a third of the money I had left from my grandfather's estate. (How could a trailer home, a garage, a lush tomato patch, and a couple of live chickens be worth so little?)

The first room had a bar, behind which a woman in a filthy sarong asked me what I wanted.

"I really need help," I said to her. A geyser of sensibility and truth erupted within me.

"Mmm," she said, obviously having lived quite a bit herself. "I can't help you with that just yet. And we don't serve liquor. But I'll give you this bubbly water for free and get back to you later."

Well. I found her comprehension of my situation quite exemplary. Who else did she look like? Like Paulette.

What else happened? All the women were tall and gawky. Some of them were definitely men in women's dresses. All of them? No. But taller, and with goofy looks in their eyes. The men tended to be short, muscular, like short Mitches. Obviously they'd been in various kinds of clinks. With a few angels in shorts and sneakers and glowing blond hair thrown in, too. I admired their humility. They all seemed like zombies to me. Oh, this is my home, I thought egregiously to myself. I wished I could concentrate more.

All right. I liked the second room and the third room. I never went upstairs that evening. In the second room a tall (I said that) woman with tangled hair was stretched on a couch with her feet in the mouth of a black man in a paisley shirt. Her foot size must have been eleven or twelve. A short, beefy truckload of a guy led around another gigantic woman. It was the Land of the Giant Women. Why didn't they call the club that instead of that other riddle of a name? Women kept sitting on my lap as I huddled in a dark corner, sipping my bubbly water. (I was in love right then with the bartendress who had handed me such a heartfelt gift.) "I like your pants, it's an invitation," one of them said. I wasn't used to any attention from anyone. So this was a true reversal. I seemed at last to have discovered my element.

I just want to get through the third room *until my master comes over!* There was a cage set up there. Can you imagine? In this basement in the middle of a city that was like a monster eating its own children? My new address? But there was never anybody in the cage. It seemed a lovely apartment to me. A man who resembled one of the advertisers in the back of one of my favorite barbershop comics with a muscular, bumpy body sat on a bench by the cage. He had his thing out of his pants. A woman, the most delicious one there except for the bartendress, was asking him question after question. "I brought my wife here, but she didn't like it," he explained to her.

For a brief moment the spell was broken. I sat myself down in a corner on a broken chair in the darkest, most inconspicuous spot I could find. Which didn't stop falsely made-up women from planting themselves on my lap. I shunted them away desperately. Perhaps I was frightened. Sitting there for a spare moment, I felt my skin tingle.

Suddenly I was scared of becoming a dead weight of a corpse like the gentleman I had so admired in the casket in the funeral home on Main Street. I loved my mother. I remembered when she used to sing me a song in a rocking chair at bedtime: "Baby, baby bunting / Uncle Willie's gone a-hunting / Dished his knife, dished his wife / He's going after the big game tonight." How I loved that lullaby! And all of the intentional kindness it took for her to sing it to me. While I traced the zombie strain (perhaps) in my blood from my father's side, I could trace a faint humanity from my mother's. Her blue padded nightgown (with the lace frills at the cuffs) on which I nestled my head in that rocking chair was like a flag of another nation. I wondered what was going on. Was this the end of the zombie road? Right here in this most unlikely pit? Had I hit bottom?

But no. No such sudden, wrenching life passage was in store for me. For as if out of the pages of an illustrated book stepped another witch doctor to only further enforce and fix my bent into a final shape. He was the man of my dreams, I mean my dream. The one who was six feet four, balding, the doctor with the syringe of death. Really. Although he was dressed simply this time, in a suit of black with a thin tie to match.

The doctor drew over a folding metal chair to sit next to my crumpled self. Edward, or Sir Edward, as he enjoyed being called, really was an M.D. I mean, he still is. His satchel was full of drugs: cocaine, poppers, ecstasy. Well, he didn't have a satchel. Let me back up. Edward pulled a folding metal chair up to the dilapidated Salvation Army wreck in which I was hunched with my bubbly drink that shot pleasurable tingles through me. It wasn't bubbly water, it turned out. It was champagne. Champagne I would gladly have drunk from the tawdry bartendress's pumps.

She actually came up to speak just as Edward squeaked his chair sideways. But his approach with his proposal was constantly interrupted. In this case by Wendy. That turned out to be her name. Her perfume lay heavily upon me. She started smoking cigarettes at me and telling me her dearest secrets, the secrets of her identity. I was stunned. She told me that she was a feminist. She told me that she used to dancc at a topless dance hall. She told me how the men who ogled her while she danced were really "passive-aggressives." She told me that I was different from the rest. She told me that when she danced the men used to fold their bills into tight origami shapes before they stuck them in her G-string so she'd have to unravel them later, causing great pain and discomfort to the joints of her lovely fingers. That's why she eventually blew that "craphole" and landed herself in this "sewer," as she described to me the lounge in which we were adrift. After I listened, I was bold enough to reiterate my need for "HELP!"

Wendy sidled up to Sir Edward. In the course of

their practically mute conversation they worked out my destiny as if they were betting on a horse. Wendy turned back to me all teary. "I'm dropping out now," she whispered soulfully. "He's better for you than me. He can blow a wind in your sails and navigate your course for you. You adorable little fucker." Then she blessed my face with kisses and bites and sweet-smelling afterthoughts. And then she was gone. My Wendy!

"I'm Sir Edward."

Edward, Sir, M.D., and so forth, was a major drug abuser, junkie. I don't think I ever saw him when something wasn't hanging out of his lips or being sucked up his fine nostrils. He was licking white powder off the backs of his fingers as he started our discourse. "So what are you experiencing?" he asked in his hollow voice. It was like a medical examination. Then he leaned back in a daze, waiting for the answer no matter how long it would take.

"Well, to tell you the truth, Sir Edward, I've been experiencing sensations quite unlike those I'm used to. I've been feeling, for a few minutes, at least, worried yet relaxed, expectant yet hopeful. My heart is breaking up."

Dr. Edward drew sharply forward at that one. His chair scraped quickly across the floor.

"Permission to speak?" I asked inexplicably, as a way perhaps to fill empty space.

But my question did not put Dr. Edward off. He was looking very concerned as he drew his face close to mine. He appeared to have the face of a horse, when seen so closely. The insides of his ears were rank with tufts of hair. He had the largest hands. The kind the old women in the Methodist church used to call "Jesus hands." Dr. Edward's really were big and heavy and transformative.

"You want a freaky pill?" he asked quietly in the murmuring, slightly aristocratic accent he usually spoke in.

I later found out he was from a town of 1,100 in Ohio where white-trash bikers banded together in militia units. He was thirty-nine years old. He had created a tangent for himself that combined his medical practice with other sorts of intervention and control. He had been walking that tangent like a plank for several years now.

Those drugs he offered me turned out to be a golden door. A few minutes before, I had felt that I was somehow at the end of my zombiehood, my very existence. I was shaken to the basement of my fragile house. But he knowingly presented me with a new path to freedom and self-expression. Drugs. Self-deluding drugs. There was a tornado set free inside my personal territory.

"You took the edge off me," I whispered to him as he sat there glowering.

"It's forbidden fruit," he answered.

"Will these drugs take over?"

"Yup."

"Wow."

I felt these were the sorts of conversations going on all around me. The curtain had been drawn again over the eye in the middle of my forehead. I was all nerve endings. And then the lights went out one by one. Wow! Drugs! I was curious about their different effects and side effects. He was sticking a vial of starry powder into my nostrils. I had nothing left but longing and helplessness. I, too, was suddenly a monster. A monster of a different persuasion.

This is what I saw. This is what I felt: a new longing. I was no longer a boy. I saw the side of my head tingle. I felt the need to be kept in a quivering sac of unending sensation of meaningless waves breaking on the shore. All straight lines became curving lines on a highway. I felt I was being driven by a smashed teen-ager on curving dirt roads at night where many had been smashed up before. Whoa! I buckled up! I was careening while grabbing on to the strap on the side. We were driving to the ocean. I peed into the salty sea underneath the interrogation of the moon. "I hope you're not doing what I think you're doing," my psychotic driver was saying to me.

"It's always going to start with you with an injection or a snort," Dr. Edward said to me. "I know you want what's on my mind. I know you like what's on my mind."

I went further into the dream.

CHAPTER 6

Sir Edward the M.D.

O H, I WAS WAITING for the needle. And then he unloaded its cargo of stars into me. There were so many asterisks. I was so far away from a real place. I am so filled with lassitude. I have to have someone out there who is going to take command of my brain. And it seems that the commands are sputters, farther and farther between. I live with Edward the M.D. probably because he has no command of my brain, so I barely see him and he barely sees me. I'm not sure why he wants this, but I can't fathom him. I think he gets control of me through drugs. He likes getting me high. So I am brought to life only from the outside. And the outside is flickering constantly to no one's satisfaction.

One day, for instance, Dr. Edward had a visitor from Virginia whose name was WSeal64735. WSeal64735 was the next person I grew to love and adore. I felt my heart immediately begin its worshiping, its spongy loving, from afar. He stood straight and tall. His pants were like harem pants made of

garish purple-and-rose patterns on a gray background. He was wearing a nylon purple jacket with
a letter on its back, the letter *V*. When he took it off
he had on a lemon-colored ribbed T-shirt that showed
his blushing, discolored muscles. His face too was discolored and acned. On his feet were big floating adhe-
sive boats of sneakers decorated with stripes as bright
as the neon of Times Square at night (one of Dr.
Edward's favorite places to walk me). His high school
ring featured a garnet stone that reminded me of the
Egyptian room so important in my own genesis.

I think he came over to buy some weed. He was
a nephew of Dr. Edward's visiting from Virginia Beach.
He was seventeen, a pro wrestler. These were his stats.
He was blond, blue eyed, five feet eleven, 170, with sev-
enteen-inch arms. Lots of this stuff he told me. He liked
to bend down and talk with me. He said I "amused"
him. (The word sounded funny coming from his broken, curving lips.) He said his hobbies were hunting,
fishing, wrestling, and "talking to Tori!!!" He liked to
write movies and worked on a local college radio station as a deejay. He told me he was "bulking up."
Whenever he didn't know what to say for a hee-haw,
like a bumper sticker on a car he'd say, "Why make
friends when war is much more satisfying?"

"What do you do?" he said, hunching down to
talk to me half-politely. (I was lying curled on a folded-
over mattress next to a dirty floor-level half window
from which I could watch people in other apartments.)

He said it as if I were a monkey or something.

"Well, WSeal64735," I started out slowly, "Dr. Edward was kind enough to take me in. I have no clue otherwise. I come from Pennsylvania. I have glimmers of something more sometimes. But I can't get there from here. What do you do?"

My response really got WSeal64735 laughing long and hard. "I'm a pro wrestler in Virginia."

"On TV?"

"No, I'm still in high school."

I knew all about pro wrestling from the TV watching I did all day and night in the apartment. "Do you have a character?" .

"The Sadistic One," he said.

"What do you mean?"

That's when he lifted up his T-shirt, which was colored as brightly as the sun and showed the adjective "Sadistic" tattooed across his belly.

"Ooooooh, it's beautiful and simple." That made him laugh some more.

By now he was bent down on his haunches in front of me. He was a male version of Jeannie of *I Dream Of Jeannie* in those billowing pants. Or he was Sinbad the sailor. "Maybe you should be called 'Sinbad,'" I offered.

"Hah!" he let out. "That would go over like a lead balloon. I'm gonna have to take you to a pro wrestling match. You can watch me. You can sit with my girlfriend, Tori."

"What's this brewing?" the good doctor asked.

By now Edward the M.D. was towering over us. Of course he towered over everyone just by standing. He merely seemed to be safeguarding his property. I felt very flattered actually that he cared to possess me. I didn't understand his motives. But then I guess he was just some other kind of creature destined to turn other people's dials just as I was destined to be a receiver rather than a transmitter.

"Don't worry, Jack," said WSeal64735 as he extended himself way up on his legs. "I'm not gonna make off with your precious slave. Although I don't know exactly what you get out of having this pet. But then I do. He's got something. A quality that makes me feel good."

"It makes me feel good, too," Edward replied with the evenness of a straightedge ruler.

"We'll share him, me and my girlfriend will share him with you, and if you don't like it I'll tell my father your brother," he said almost threateningly. I don't know what ancient power struggle lurked behind the threat.

"I've been shared by a criminal, male, and his friend, female, before," I piped up. "It ended badly."

"How badly?" WSeal64735 demanded.

"I was arrested in the funeral parlor by cops holding a smoking gun, and my father put me on a bus for New York City."

"And who did you meet in New York?"

WSeal64735 asked boastfully. Then he answered his own question. "Me!"

"Oh yes," I concurred.

"Anyway, you can come with us if you want, Edward. I'm just gonna take him to a pro wrestling match."

"Agreed."

"You little dweeb," were the last words of WSeal64735 before he did the strangest thing. He picked me up. He started throwing my arms upwards so that I couldn't grab onto myself or protect my body and face. Then he started swatting me. Then he smashed me up against the blue-and-white-striped wallpaper until I could practically hear my bones crack. Then he pushed my ribs repeatedly. I felt like Jerry Lewis in a movie I watched on TV where he kept tumbling down the same palace stairs over and over. Wow. I was actually bloody in the face. I couldn't believe sweet, lovable WSeal64735 was laying into me so harshly. Did he know Mark?

"I'm just knocking some sense into you," whispered WSeal64735. Then the strangest thing happened. He collapsed in a corner and buried his face in his hands, weeping.

"I'm just knocking some love into you," he added in a crackling, imploring whimper.

"Needless to say, our family has been witness to some wild scenes," said Edward the M.D. from a far corner, where he stood on a stepladder, fashioning into a hangman's noose a black rope that always hung there.

"Is that for me?" I blubbered.

"Not if you stick to your destiny. Especially because you don't understand your destiny. And you have to follow it blindly and deeply. While others walk the earth like pedestrians following the 'Walk-Don't Walk' signs."

"Jesus," I managed.

"Hardly. . . . Here, let's get you dressed for bed."

Dr. Edward retrieved from the redwood closet my straitjacket made of tan burlap. He helped me into its confining stiff-collar ambience. He wrapped my arms over themselves with the oversize sleeves. He then laid me under the black hangman's noose. He lowered the noose with a cranking wheel, which was like a navigator's wheel at the helm of a ship. Then he loosened the black oblong so that it fit over my head and he secured that as loosely as a tie about my neck. Then he left me for dead. I slept that night like a baby. The only disturbances were the snores of WSeal64735 alseep in the corner.

Chapter 7
The pro wrestling match.

THE TRIP TO DAYTON, OHIO, went smoothly. The bus came and went on time. It was much like the bus I had taken from Pennsylvania months earlier. It had screens on which movies played, so I was quite comfortable. Only the smell of the other people was slightly overpowering. Dr. Edward sat next to me, reading a dictionary. He always said, "Why not go to the source?" explaining that he felt that since books were made of various words, why not just read the one book that included all of them.

"Who's the fucking asshole around here?" WSeal64735 asked loudly from across the aisle. He never did explain what he meant by that.

He was sitting there with Tori, his girlfriend from Virginia, who was accompanying us on this odyssey. It was apparently a very important yearly match, from what WSeal64735 said. Tori was a young woman, big breasts, dyed blond hair, in an oversize gray sweatshirt, black pedal pushers, and white pumps that allowed us to see her toenails painted bright pink. She obviously loved me. And she obviously feared WSeal64735. I could tell.

"Oh, Zombie," she would sing from across the aisle, "tell us what you're thinking."

Whenever I did she would laugh. She obviously wasn't smart enough to pick up on the more serious repercussions of some of my jabs. But I loved her nevertheless. She reminded me a bit of Mother back in Pennsylvania, the way she could be so sweet smelling, the way she never hit me like my father or the other boys. But women do definitely hit. I learned that around Sir Edward's house, where different women would visit who would carry riding crops and cat-o'-nine-tails to swipe at the butterscotch behinds of businessmen who paid them on the way out. Dr. Edward often went for a walk during these ventings. I was unnoticeable enough that no one cared if I stayed or if I went.

We stayed at a motel in Dayton. It was a standard deal with a cot for me.

The event was anything but standard. The stadium was filled for the celebratory event. Fireworks went off inside the dome of the palace of sweat. Laser lights of red, white, and blue vivisected the air. Little boys imitated their big bears of fathers by wearing caps with brims and hooting at the cameras while making air fists. Little girls imitated bigger girls by dyeing their hair blond and wearing lots of dark tan makeup and bright red or even purple lipstick. Their lips matched the rockets' red glare.

Our row was delightful. We sat on benches. Edward the M.D. sat as tall as a coat rack at one end. He resembled Abraham Lincoln, so ugly and cold and tall. He had shot himself with some drug he said would fortify the calcium in his bones. It mainly seemed to fill his eyes with a blurry white dust. Then me. I held a smile on my face for the entire three hours. I couldn't help it. WSeal64735 sat next to me with his arm around my shoulder for the duration. He was dressed in the same sort of harem pants and yellow shirt I remembered from the first time I laid eyes on him. Every time someone was bashed in the rectangular, roped-off stage in the middle, he would squeeze me or smack me. I felt as if the entire match were being broadcast telepathically to me through his arms and oversize hands. On his other side, wrapped in his other arm, was Tori, his beloved Tori. She kept complaining.

"This is a dumb sport. It's not a sport. It's all posing. How can these people be so dumb as to fall for this shit? It's an insult to my intelligence."

"Shut up. It's my profession."

I felt empathy for WSeal64735 at that moment. I felt that he was hurt by what Tori was saying. It was as if he were showing her his heart and soul reflected in a mirror and she was dismissing him. I hurt bad for him. I wondered if he were siphoning those feelings into me as a way to relieve himself. I was the perfect sponge for WSeal64735. I felt as if I were suffering so that he could feel full and powerful and free.

First matched were Flyin' Brian and Alex Wright. Flyin' Brian paraded into the arena dressed in black-and-white fringed pants and a jacket like Davy Crockett's but dipped in black ink instead of being brown and furry like a squirrel's. His curly blond locks tumbled down over his shoulders. He weighed 234 pounds and was announced to be living now in Hollywood, California. He was unshaved. He adored the glory obviously of standing in the ring. He air-filmed a girl in the audience to signal that he had the hots for her. Her face was a bony and angular violin case. Then arrived Alex Wright, who was being promoted as "the youngest pro wrestler in Nuremberg, Germany." He wore a black leather jacket over his skimpy red briefs. He wore tall black construction boots as well. He slunk off the black leather jacket to toss into the face of an umpire who was dressed in a midnight blue suit, his hair as white as snow, his demeanor that of a preacher man. WSeal64735 explained to me that Alex was "a pretty boy" and "a punk."

Their match turned out to be dramatic, an endlessly grueling gyration for position. They held each other's heads in squeezes. They kept making each other slide their ball sacs along the wire ropes. They somersaulted each other off the stage onto the brutal tarmac. Once Alex flew through the air to land in a swoop on Brian. Eventually Alex upset the men, but he seemed to draw the appreciation of the younger women by winning. When he won he shimmied and roared in another language, German. I was rooting for him when he was winning. (And for Brian when he was winning.) I wanted to shake his hand in congratulations as Flyin' Brian was doing. But when he spoke, or emoted, outside the parameters of violence, he seemed somehow embarrassing. He made me think of the curious windshield wiper of a man on the bus who had farted on his way to the men's station at the rear.

The second match was a tag team event with the Hollywood Blonds, consisting, again, of Flyin' Brian, and Stunnin' Steven, with a much shorter haircut than Brian's, versus the Four Horsemen, represented by Iron Man Anderson and Paul Roma. Stunnin' Steve wore a black bikini with a beautiful red star on his behind. Flyin' Brian obviously was very fond of his partner because he kissed him on the lips when they met on the margins. The fatter the ladies on the perimeter, the jollier they seemed to become when confronted with either a kiss or a punch. Flyin' Brian then made an air camera pointed at the audience.

"Hollywood Blonds are Sylvester Stallone's favorite team," WSeal64735 explained to me. He was very talkative and explanatory during this match and the next.

"Iron Man Anderson is the Zsa Zsa Gabor of wrestling," he said. "He's had seven tag team partners. As many partners as she's had husbands." Then he let out a fart of laughter.

The game was a bit hard to follow with four in the ring instead of two. Flyin' Brian with the curly locks and the hairy chest was at his best when his opponent was down or hurt. Then he'd produce as if out of a magic hat the most startling backhanded slaps. He'd throw his opponent into the iron railing below so that the only view the loser had was of pairs and pairs of cheap footwear.

"He's like a shark," WSeal64735 told me. "When the blood's on the water he goes into a frenzy."

The Hollywood Blonds won.

Next up: Ravishing Rick Rude opposed The Natural. I have to admit that I fell in love with the audacity of Rick Rude. He had the mustache of Clark Gable. He mouthed off like Mae West. He wore the clothes of Liberace. I'd seen them all on late-night TV. He strutted onto the plank and onto the square of the spotlit stage beyond in a blue-sequined bathrobe covered with white glitter. On the rear of his bathrobe, the sort boxers wear, was the legend *Simply Ravishing*. When he arrived onstage, Rick Rude instructed the audience from the mike: "Shut your mouth. Open your eyes. Show some respect to the next champion. Hit the music." The song was "We Are the Champions" by the rock group Queen.

"What a man!" WSeal64735 strangely exulted to me while Rick Rude simulated a hula hoop movement as his 261-pound adversary approached with his dyed white hair. I didn't like him nearly as much. "He looks like a big fat Texas steer in heat," WSeal64735 complained. Those were my feelings exactly. I felt moved that we both were rooting for the same champion. Tori didn't have a clue. Edward the M.D. had been to the men's room and back. His eyes were sparkling from the fresh implosion of drugs.

The struggle between the two pro wrestlers proved to be agonizing. Rick Rude began tormenting his opponent very early, apparently much too early, according to my overbearing, guiding friend, WSeal64735. He spat on him. He yelled, "How you like it, boy?" when he was down. He blew snot on his back and belly. "That's what they call 'the farmer's handkerchief,'" WSeal64735 explained. "Because farmers don't have handkerchiefs in the fields." Then Mr. Rude put the Natural into what is called a "deep freeze." He squeezed his arm around his neck so tightly that his eyes bulged red, his face paled, his body fell limp. Bugles were played through the sound system.

"Look at the eyes. He's going to dreamland," WSeal64735 offered. But soon enough, of course, everything turned around. The Natural wasn't a true zombie. I knew it. He returned from dreamland. I never would have. He did this. He did that. It was a draw, something called "a double dq."

On the way home in the bus we all sat on the long bench at the rear. I slept on WSeal64735's broad shoulder. Dr. Edward was on my left, Tori on WSeal64735's right. I knew that I had picked up a new habit in Dayton and it wouldn't go away. Once we got home I sat in front of the television whenever a pro wrestling match was broadcast. The new habit never went away as long as I lived there. I had all these enthusiastic feelings. Recently I'd been reading a lot in a paperback about trans-species communication. That made me feel very emotional, too.

"Do you think my muscles might shrink from no exercise?" I asked WSeal64735 one afternoon as we both lay on the floor, watching a match between Sting and Lex Luger.

"Naw," he replied. "The kind of exercise I do isn't that kind, anyway. My last match I got hit in the ribs with a chair, and I've still got bruised ribs. I've been resting for a month from my kinda exercising. Soon I've got a rematch with him. I have a new tag team partner, though. His name is Genocide. He's six feet four and weighs 230 pounds. I'm going to do wrestling full-time come this summer."

Those were the kinds of talks we had lying on the linoleum throughout the long winter. I knew I had stumbled into a lucky corridor. I didn't know how long it would last. It lasted a long time. But then the inevitable happened. Dr. Edward returned one afternoon upset by a drug that had an opposite effect to that intended. He was poisoned. He took out the terrible side effects on my big, dearest WSeal64735, sliced his throat until the blood was caked on the linoleum and all the buxom life was forced from him. I began to mourn and heave and weep. It was as if I were reborn as something else by his death. I felt nothing but horror and dread from this terrible cheap murder, this piece of tabloidism. I love tabloids. They are my only source of news. But I like them because they bring into my living room another life. Now here in the void of every scary emotion I ever felt was the dead body of my dear teenage pro wrestler. That was tragedy! That was not comedy! I was heaving from the confrontation with nothingness like a big embryonic zero in my own belly. My shoes were loose, but my head was on tight. Oh God!

What happened then was that Edward the M.D. was holding out two tablets for me, plastic medicinal tablets of half red and half green. "These Tylenols will make you forget everything you've seen," he instructed severely. I recognized them from the local pharmacy where I shopped for lottery tickets. I took them. I swallowed the lie. I pretended never to remember again that moment of apple-slashing horror when the throat of my one true friend was cut and a potentially powerful career was stuffed into a suitcase and put into the trash for good. He inserted the suitcase in a clear blue bag so that it would go out with the biodegradable garbage, luckily the murder taking place on the proper night for the blue rather than the green bag, and I suppose in that way somehow concealed his horror in the ecosystem. This city, I discovered, wasn't as much fun as it used to be. I was growing up. I was determined to make the most of the bitterness for as long as I could. Hoping that there would be a turn in the road up ahead. Maybe not the final turn, but a brief one where I would meet the almightly God who rules heaven and earth. But I also knew that that was not yet.

I guess that's just the way it goes. If you look alive, you'll be taken away and tried. I am living in the prison of the world. I can't believe it's come to this squeeze. I wish my parents hadn't abandoned me. I sometimes pretend to wish that I hadn't abandoned them. But then that's not the way it happened.

Chapter 8

How Zombie went scuba diving.

ONE FINE EVENING Edward the M.D. returned in a fouler mood than usual.

"I've had it with this fucking town," he cursed so loudly that I woke up, the TV still on with the third talk show of the afternoon. "Nobody pays up. Everybody's a vampire. Everybody sucks my ever-living blood dry."

I didn't know what he was talking about. I felt that it was some sort of confusion in the delivery and prescription and payment of particular neurological drugs in which he claimed to specialize. Though I never did actually see his office. Or see him in a white doctor's shirt. I acquiesced just to acquiesce.

"So I'm gonna take us on a vacation. You ever go on a vacation?"

I didn't know what Sir Edward the M.D. was talking about. It was all wrong. The words in my head were still continuing on their spool of endless spinning. There was no vacation.

"Nice shot," I said back to him innocently. But

he didn't take it so innocently. He started to make me endure the longest, worst thrashing with long, big black straps all bound together into a single black leather wing. The sensation was of complete oblivion, again.

"They stick it in your face and let you smell what they consider wrong," he was howling above me in a continuous shriek. That's what I mean about it not being satisfying or leading anywhere. I mean, what was he talking about? When did people start talking like this? And the thing about words is they don't lead anywhere. Unless they're to put a spell on someone.

"You deserve to go down with me to the Caribbean!" he shouted.

"Okay," I cried.

Pretty soon he was calm, cool, and collected again, making reservations with a travel agent who would allow us to take our scuba vacation in the Caribbean.

I particularly missed WSeal64735 the morning of our departure. I remembered how he had taken care of me on the bus to Dayton, Ohio. How his body odor smelled more of frankincense than that of the other people. How big and loud and overprotective he had been. Traveling with Edward the M.D. was like traveling with a mortician. Sir Edward was as upright as a board and dressed all in black. In the apartment he fit in better. In the airport everybody stared at him. I think it was the black leather pants and boots and vest under the short black raincoat that added to his shady difference from everybody else. I don't know what I looked like in my shorts and dirty white baseball cap, dragging the cart loaded with black lockers full of equipment for diving. Sir Edward said that he didn't trust the equipment they provided at a resort. It could be full of leaks and germs and other imperfections.

There was never any love lost between me and Dr. Edward. Maybe that's why we got along as long as we did. I was relieved in the plane when he sat far forward in the first-class section, separated from the rest of us by a hanging velvet curtain. I sat in the last seat all the way back. Luckily it was a seat separated off by itself. Its only limitation was that it didn't shift backward like all the other seats. I had to sit bolt upright. The little square of window next to me was a great amusement. I watched endlessly as the clouds were erased on the blackboard of the sky, only to be re-created again in a dusty phantasmagoria. I remembered skywriting planes from when I was a young thumb of a boy in Pennsylvania. I remembered a skywriting plane. Its message: "Smoke Kents."

A bus, a van: the transition to the double room at the resort was a long, complicated affair: a bus, a van. The next thing I knew I was lying on the stone floor of our room. Every so often an iguana would crawl up the wall or a giant water bug would scuttle across the floor next to me. There were two double beds. One was reserved for the giant trunks with all of Edward the M.D.'s clothes and our own equipment. Everything Edward the M.D. brought was black: black military shorts, black T-shirts, black combat boots, a black suit from an expensive store, a black hooded sweatshirt for the sun, lots of black reflector sunglasses. The equipment looked as if it had been ransacked from a laboratory: hoses, silver tubes, masks. He had even brought along two tanks filled with compressed air. Edward slept in his black socks and black-and-white polka-dotted boxers. All the lights were left burning all night long. Just like at home.

The morning rose gradually over the terrace. Sir Edward the M.D. and I went to breakfast on a stone terrace filled with others. Lots were foul-mouthed policemen and firemen who were forcing their wives to dive with them because of the "buddy system," which allows for diving only with a "buddy." They made their frightened wives participate. I was filling in for Edward the M.D. Luckily what we discovered on the vacation was that no creature was better fitted for such a sport than yours truly.

When questioned at the deck, Edward the M.D. swore "on the Koran," as he put it—inscrutably to the attendants—that I had my scuba-diving license. He gave them fake numbers and dates to send them off on a chase for a certificate that didn't exist. He did indeed have his own certification for open-water diving, either authentic or fake, I never did discover. While other blowhards, as well as pleasant people from Holland, Germany, and the United States, climbed onto group boats equipped with lots of sleek, safe air tanks, to be transported to lovely dive sites, Sir Edward had chartered his own long boat to drop us in the center of a pretty blank uncharted scratch of water off an uninhabited island called Klein Bonaire. All we had was our driver, who spoke Papiamento, a local language comprising Spanish, Portuguese, and an African dialect brought along by salt-harvesting slaves in the early nineteenth century. He spoke broken English as well.

We had only antiquated equipment. I put on my helmet of black metal with big nuts and bolts around its neck that Sir Edward screwed somehow into matching outlets on my shoulders. I was dressed in a black leather wet suit that was puffed up by an air-enhancing device attached to the side. My webbed feet were black as well. They were tipped with aluminum. "So you can see them in the underwater sunlight," Sir Edward told me. He was dressed in an identical outfit. I wished at that moment we were going snorkeling instead. He then burdened me with an air tank painted black instead of the pretty yellows, blues, and reds of those who had hooted so merrily on the tourist boats. He reassured me that ours were mixed with a special spiking of nitrogen so that we could go down deeper for longer. The only danger was something called "nitrogen narcosis," which meant that the excess nitrogen combined with oxygen deprivation led to some kind of ecstasy, similar to the feeling from the drugs he'd shoot me up with, but often followed, unfortunately, if I remember correctly, by bends and eruptions of arteries.

I'd always been so sportless. But after I was pushed off the boat backward, holding my mask to my eyes and nose and my oxygen hose to my mouth, I found myself descending into a zone of increasingly difficult and stultifying and seductive pressure. It was as if I'd been wrapped in duct tape and pushed into a bank vault where the pressure was increased by hundreds of psi's every few moments. I was completely alone under the lit surface of the sea. My head felt as if it were exploding outward like an unhappy circus balloon. I bit on the hose in my mouth, sucking down hard on the compressed air. Farther and farther away until the boat was just like the shadow of a leaf on the green blue roof of water above. My breathing played back to me, greatly amplified. What kind of sport was this? It was like a burial at sea, all those boxes filled with unfortunate sailors drifting slowly and irregularly through the iridescent blue to the shadier depths below as colors gradually became lost on the descent: first red, then yellow and blue. I loved the improbable nothingness of this "sport."

The true beauty of it, though, was the bigness. Dense water makes things seem bigger and closer. Big fish would begin to look at me. Once I was drifting along with a school of muscular yellow fishes. Then suddenly I felt silly to be one of them. Just then I noticed another fish, a gray fish, glance up at me as if he were feeling the same thing. He dropped out of the undulating flock. So did I. Had he really looked at me? I loved communicating with the fish. It was a ticklish pleasure to look at the fish who were smaller than me with their flirtatious eyes with the long lashes and their yellow and green and lavender skins. But it was a trivial feeling of fun. Something else entirely was meeting in the magnifying waters the fish whose bodies were bigger than mine. I first met a giant silver fish longer by twice than me. His eyes were slanted. His whole body was shoulders and hips, the tail swishing gigantically from side to side. I felt my heart try to hide within its own pulsing, yet the more it tried to hide, the more it was forced up into my throat. It was as if I were throwing up my heart juices. But I lived.

As I continued on my journey I soon found myself on the floor of the dirty brown ocean. Most color had now been left behind. All was like a sepia photograph. But there was a beautiful spiritual stillness to the grouping I felt drawn to join. Other scuba divers who had been diving in other groups in all sorts of gear were now congealed, kneeling on the floor of the ocean with their backs lined against a sort of grotto, as if a half shell had been set on its side fashioned out of phosphorescent mud. That's the closest I can come to trying to communicate its texture to you who live above the line. I found an empty spot and knelt along with them. Suddenly! from above! was lowered a sort of electric fence on which were sloppily tied different pieces of fish meat. It was a graph in which certain squares were stuffed with abstract slices and hunks of ragged meat and others left vacant. It was a mathematical god of flesh and design being lowered from above. I wondered if this were a religion of the god Fish I had not yet encountered.

I was right, if you allow some leverage to that last remark. Suddenly in a splutter these amazing sharks—they were sharks, I knew that, I'd seen movies—descended. There must have been twenty or thirty exploding into the sacred area of water where we were, I thought, worshiping the sacrifices of yellowtail tuna and red snapper. They went into such a frenzy of feeding that I thought I'd die with admiration and fear and disgust and curiosity. It was more emotion than I'd ever felt at one time, all adding up to what I began to think of as a religious experience. That's where I locate my rekindling of interest in that childhood feeling of awe I'd had in the Scranton museum that had never been matched before or since. The sharks weren't God. But they were, I suppose, angels. And when they were finished they left silently. Though I wondered why they had spared us. Is that why we were kneeling? Was it really just a show we wanted? Dunno. There are others more able than me to divulge those secrets.

I did swim along farther on this loveliest of dives. That's when I saw the dolphins. They broke my heart. Unlike the sharks, who have such a bad reputation, they, who have such a lovely reputation, carried on shamelessly. There in the darker depths I watched what I knew to be bottlenose dolphins killing porpoises. It was a very helter-skelter scene. The bottlenose dolphins were about ten feet long and weighed a ton. The littler porpoises were probably five feet long. Within the crazy corral of homicide the horrifying, thrilling, and stupid display of coordinated attacks involved the bigger sweet fish attacking the necks of the smaller sweet fish, then ramming their internal organs, then gashing their silvery necks with their teeth. I felt as if I were hiding behind a car, watching a gangland murder. They didn't even seem to derive any advantage from their victims, who simply rose to the top to eventually be washed ashore. I heard talk of careless fishermen, but no, I'd witnessed the rubout, yet I was too lost and too indifferent to report. It was beautiful to be at a murder site without any culpability.

Eventually I rose to the top. I was in pain the entire time. I'd practically run out of air. Luckily I breathe so superficially normally that I possessed double the amount of compressed air of most of the remaining divers. Still, the marker on my depth gauge was well in the red. I'd known nothing but worship for nearly an hour at ninety feet below. I felt nothing but the uncomfortable rack of my own body. I was like the rack hung with fish flesh waiting to be eaten by sharks. The pain was in my lower spine. I felt like a fish hooked by its own spine. All the supernatural splendor I'd seen disappeared when I equalized and emptied the water from my visor.

Sir Edward the M.D. couldn't have been more furious. If he could have paced the decks of the boat, he would have. But it was such a small rowboat of a yacht that instead he just stumbled from side to side in his black suit, smoking the dregs of a thin, mean, white cigarette. I'm not sure why he was so angry. I think he sensed that I had experienced some power and specialness in the depths of which he had been deprived. Normally he would have ridiculed my achievement. It certainly fit. Where else could you be mummified and lowered into a claustrophobic watery prison and have it be considered an athletic achievement? But everything was reversed in this marvelous resort we'd come to.

"I should send you back to the pet store," he snarled.

I knew then that my days with Sir Edward the M.D. were numbered.

Chapter 9

Zombie's departure from
Sir Edward the M.D.'s house.

I LAY ON THE FLOOR day after tedious day, waiting for the other shoe to drop. Waiting for him to come stomping in in a furious fit. Waiting for him to throw a dagger at me or a glass that would shatter at my forehead, something like that. Instead there was just this simmering, horrible stillness. He didn't look at me or tie my noose at the end of the night so I could sleep. He just pretended over and over again that I simply wasn't there. Other times when he ignored me he was really ignoring me. These times when he ignored me I felt he was pretending to ignore. I felt the pressure of intention that had been absent between us before, when I was truly a nonperson to him. Now he was just pretending. What had happened? I would never know. His moods were so pharmaceutical that they were beyond me. I had no medical degree and had never worked behind a counter in a drugstore.

I took advantage of the fake peace, however. Especially when it was real peace and he was out of the house, which was almost every afternoon, almost every evening. At night he threw every glass object he touched—against the wall, through the window, but never at me. In the mornings he slept with his eyes rolled up in his head. I then tried to remain unde-tected, breathing as shallowly as possible, remember-ing what I had learned on the floor of the sea when the sharks were ravaging above. When he dressed and went out "to the park," then I would allow myself to rouse. I would drink cups and cups of Coca-Cola from a giant bottle of the rust-colored liq-uid he kept in the refrigerator. Then I would turn on the TV and come to life.

Indeed, it was during those fragile days that the miracle occurred. I was pushing the cable buttons when I came across the show of Control Freak. His name was printed in Magic Marker on a piece of cardboard that ran beneath his face like the numbers of a criminal in a police photo-portrait. He was oper-ating the videocamera himself. It was quite a primi-tive operation, really. His face was narrowly framed so you could never see his body or his setting. He could have been on another planet. He would talk—rant, really—on and on, unshaved but never having a true beard or mustache, just shady, with a big nose. He was losing his hair, but it was still there in all its ragged inkiness. I'd put him in his early thirties. His show took place on one of the stations far to the end of the numbers, approaching channel 100, maybe it was channel 99. Just when you were getting interested, everything would flicker and the show would go dead. But a big placard would appear to shakily fill the screen (obviously handheld) with the number to call and he would call you back. One day I got it together to copy down the number. I wrote it on my stomach with one of Dr. Edward's special thick pencils that sometimes hung about his neck on a string.

So I began to tune in every day around three o'clock in the afternoon. It was my favorite time of day, just when the videotronic weather of the television became most predictable. It was unpredictable in the main stations to the left of the box. But when you began to approach the right, there was nothing like it except perhaps at five or six in the morning. But then it was the sheer, obvious wackiness of an American flag blowing in the breeze to the sound of the bugles playing, or an infomercial with a Shakespearean actor demonstrating a potato chopper. But this was a time of day when weirdness slipped somehow into normalcy, I think perhaps the kids were almost ready to get home from school, maybe some were there already, early for the afterschool specials, but you couldn't be sure. That's when Control Freak would show up again in all his grayness. (He obviously couldn't afford color.)

I'm nervous about even trying to approach his message because I don't have the exact words in front of me in any kind of typescript. Control Freak

liked to talk about many things. I of course wanted
to call him, but I knew if I gave him Sir Edward the
M.D.'s home number and the tall, mean monster
himself picked up the receiver, I would be literally
dead rather than just half-dead. On the day of the
miracle he talked and talked about the deity who
lived at the bottom of the stairs in the cellar of the
universe and ran everything meanly and rancorously.
I recognized in his description my personal view of
how things were going. Oh my God! Maybe his was
the address of my true identity!

One thing he was probably trying to do was to
lure women to swoon at his funky image and call
him up—sticking a worm on a hook and letting it
drop into gray space so that women would respond.
He obviously felt the need for hot wax on which he
could stamp the seal of his intellectual royalness. I
mean, it was just all words. His face hardly ever
changed. It all took place in a tight-cropped, close
frame. Maybe everybody imagined their own idyllic
setting for this man with the tall forehead (as tall as
Edward the M.D.'s). How did he get the money to
pay for the time? He seemed peculiarly entrancing
because of the neediness of his reaching out of the
frame of the TV. His hands were so big, they seemed
to want to get out of the frame.

On that day I kept tiptoeing up to and back
from what the Control Freak had to say. "I can't help
but conclude that much that is considered darkness

is just really the motor of who we are . . . I think you'd be better off if you were dead."

Wow! The passion of his delivery certainly surpassed anything he'd done on the air so far. Just my luck Sir Edward the M.D. had to walk in at that moment. It was the moment of truth.

"How dare you use up my cable time?" he said.

Then he started in on me. On us, really. First he broke the television screen with a bat he'd borrowed from the landlady. Then he turned to face me. He rarely faced me fully frontally.

"But remember the waitress who brought us together?" I pleaded. "She is my protectress. I want her here if you're going to challenge me."

"You idiot," he snarled.

It started up again. A quiet beating. A beating in which you could hear the stars. I could describe every lump and thump. But who cares? For a moment we were happily carried beyond the beltway of the moon and stars to regions where few humans ever go. But the importance of such a beating is not the climactic event itself. Who hasn't been beaten? By a dad? Or a mom? Or a teacher? Or a boyfriend? Or a girlfriend? We all know the test of the fierceness of this natural event is the aftermath. Because then you return to earth with the stigmata: the black eye, the ruptured organ that requires sutures, the bleeding that leaves a stain on the skin.

That was the condition in which I finally left Sir

Edward the M.D.'s house on a charming little street in the West Village. The trees that day were flourishing from the temperate heat. It was April. The birds were singing in the trees as if they had a recording contract. And I had been cast out again.

But this time at least I had a direction. My direction was toward the Control Freak. He was a good voodoo master, I could tell. I had his number written on my stomach.

Chapter 10

Control Freak.

BY NOW I WAS USED to being thrown out of places. Edward the M.D. too had abandoned me to wandering the streets of downtown Manhattan, where it seemed just when a window looked particularly friendly the lights would be put out. I spent a couple of nights sleeping in doorways, smelling the shish kebab cooking in Middle Eastern concession stands.

Then I called the number I'd scrawled on my tummy.

"This is Control Freak," said the deep, hollow, baritone voice speaking from the depths of the handset. "Leave me your number and I'll call you when I feel like it."

I read the number off the booth's phone into the speaker, then hung up. I was on a corner near a square park with a triumphal arch at its entrance. Dried colored leaves were falling. The phone booth was a pod of potential information, a tetrahedron of glass. The leaves kept falling. No one called.

Different sorts of people kept stepping into its solitude to refresh themselves with a phone call. Some left offerings of nickels or dimes by mistake. They did not know that I was suffering nearby, waiting. What if Control Freak kept receiving busy signals? Would he ever call again? Or was it one strike you're out? I was so happy, so attenuated. The suspense excited me. The sun was at ten o'clock, then noon, then soon at four o'clock, then six. There's no hope for the hopeless.

Finally the call I had been waiting for came through the wires.

"Zombie?" he asked, his voice smaller and drier, more of a wind instrument than on TV.

"Yes, sir," I replied quickly.

"What's your scene?" he asked.

"I'm lost, sir," I answered. "I have no place to live. I was told by a hypnotist who was a friend of my last host, Sir Edward the M.D., that I'm the easiest subject for hypnosis he ever experienced."

"Why are you telling me that?"

"I had a hunch you might want to hypnotize me in some way. I'm a huge fan of your show. Do you have any use for a fan?"

"Now you're talking. You must have some psychic powers to have said such a thing. Because the only thing I need is a fan. Otherwise I'm self-sufficient."

"I guess I can thank my lucky stars."

"You don't have any lucky stars," he growled.

Our curious conversation continued for a long time until he finally said:

"Here's my address."

I remembered it on the long spring walk to the neighborhood I later learned was called "Tribeca." I felt as if I were carrying a paper cup of water through a storm in the desert. Then I was there. I would soon forget the outside because of the endless intricacy and trippy fascination of all that lay inside.

I traveled up the freight elevator. Stood in front of a painted black metal door. I was wearing a striped shirt, like a pajama shirt, some crinkled white khakis, sneaks. It was an outfit a boy might wear, or a clown. What a surprise when Control Freak finally answered the door, after a wait following my knocks of about a half hour. On TV I'd seen only the black cropped hair, the Italianate nose, the black dots for eyes. But in real life he was a bodybuilder, the kind featured in the pages of *Muscle and Fitness* magazine, which I often read at the magazine shop. He looked like a gila monster turned into a human. Of course I understood immediately without a conversation that the ultimate control was for him to bend and squeeze and mold his own cells and vascularity into the exact shape he desired. He was putty in his own hands.

"I love you," I said quickly, just to establish a rapport.

Control Freak didn't say anything back. He stood there, his hands gripping the sides of his opened flannel shirt. He wore short blue denim shorts cut above the thighs and a black studded belt, partly unclasped, its cheap metal buckle falling down like a serpent's head. His body was the orangest I'd ever seen. His body was actually umber. And covered in a glistening layer of sweat. He had somehow artificially arrived at the color of raw meat. The sinews of his muscles were snakes wrapped around each other in undulation. There were more veins mapped on his arms, and on the tree trunks of his thighs, than I had ever seen on a human. He reminded me of the Invisible Man statue that had been one of my dearest possessions in my bedroom in Pennsylvania when I was young. You could see all the pink organs and blue arteries and red veins. The skin of Control Freak was a battle map, or a road map.

Hardest of all, though, was the hammer of his head. He definitely did not have a sense of humor. His little eyes pierced meanly from under flying eyebrows. He was constantly atomized in a sweat of his own making. He never totally shaved. His ears were little and pointed and stuck to the sides of his head. His hair would probably have made great waves of black Latin beauty if he had allowed it to grow instead of enforcing a barbershop compliancy. Indeed, something about him reminded me of my old friends Mitch and Walt, whom I first met in the barbershop. I love when things come back. I said his head was a hammer because he reminded me of a hammerhead shark. (I knew about such things from scuba. Heh-heh.) He also reminded me of a hammerhead rattlesnake I saw a photograph of in an encyclopedia. I wouldn't want to find him waiting for me in my mailbox. But mainly I couldn't stop looking at him. It's the fascination that made me tune in whenever possible to his cable show. He was endlessly watchable, like a hypnotist's watch that swings back and forth, back and forth. His body and entire demeanor and lizard eyes were all part of the golden watch effect as he had reinvented it or discovered it for himself.

I slumped down on the floor of the hallway before his door and before the statue of himself at that moment. I still had lots of thoughts I of course could never, would never, voice. What were they? I thought that maybe it was better to have a living god than one you couldn't see. All this idolatry was really a sweet, friendly, inspiring thing. The more gods the better. The more to worship, the happier, the fuller. But I still knew that he was just the ambassador of something more even than him, of which he was merely the embodiment. I knew that I would learn more if I stuck around. I had more thoughts, but they quickly disappeared through the sieve of my fainting self. I was overcome, as I had been at the Everhart Museum the first time.

"Get up," he said sensibly, with an accent I'd come to recognize as inflected with the outer boroughs of New York City.

So I followed Control Freak into his lair. I actually crawled after him as if on an invisible leash. It was easy to continue my thoughts in such a compromising position. I was escaping to the middle of things. I thought of the humans walking outside on the streets, the ones who had been using the telephone booth for pedestrian purposes while I was awaiting my destiny. And then I thought of us, me and Control Freak. He had found his identity in something almost mythological. He had decided to become a superhero. I had decided nothing. But if I had tried to fight my destiny as a mindless zombie, what horrible consequences might have ensued. Instead of a chain I would have had a phone, instead of a cage a one-bedroom apartment with a washer and a dryer down the hall and a chute for the garbage. I'm happier floating down the river of forgetfulness with Control Freak as the indifferent current. And he's happier with my dead weight to remind him of his own importance. At least that's what I'd gleaned from his programs. You see, I felt I knew him quite well from having delved so loyally into his programming. He didn't know me so well. But he also could care less. I could see where his thoughts were from just looking about.

The room smelled of yeast. Control Freak had

every kind of powder in a tin for the effortless building of corpuscles that had been invented, and some that he'd invented himself. It was all freaky Tiger's Milk products. In the center of the loft was the bed from which Control Freak broadcast. It was a rectangular stage. A videocam was pointed straight from the bottom of the bed toward the pillows at the top. Surprisingly, we viewers had never seen that entire panorama. He would sit in a lotus position for the filming. But now I could see, to my thrill as a fan of the show, that there were actually full-length mirrors all over the nearby walls. Not much else. Control Freak kept a photograph of his girlfriend, Karen, on a sideboard. He was particularly anxious that I dust her picture daily. I'm not sure why.

The kitchen was a trip. Oat flakes filled a glass cylinder. Cartons of orange juice were lined up in the refrigerator like toy soldiers. The pills filled what must have been twenty-one bottles, each of which smelled like yeast. Many Twinlab products were there to help with low-calorie lean mass stimulation, fat free, no sugar added. Snickers bars. Over the sink was a banner on which was sewn "Everybody Hits the Wall. Some Don't Stop There." Control Freak insisted that anything served from the kitchen, including omelets fashioned only from the whites of eggs, be covered with flecks of granola.

One of Control Freak's favorite dishes, which he taught me to cook and which I made over and over again, was "yams 'n' apples." First I peeled yams and apples. Cored the apples. Then I thinly sliced the yams and apples, slicing the apples thicker than the yams. I tossed them together in a medium-size bowl. I transferred the yams and apples into a steamer pot and poured orange juice over them. I sprinkled them with raisins or cranberries and then cinnamon. I cooked until tender, approximately twenty to twenty-five minutes. Just before serving, I sprinkled Equal over the top. The whole thing, as Control Freak repeated to me every time I made this dish, came to 124 calories, 1.25 grams of protein, 29 grams of carbohydrate, 0.33 grams of fat.

The best, though, was some sort of steroid treatment. I was never explained the incidentals. I never am. But I was instructed to carry over a silver tray that contained a beautiful jabber, which he then stuck into the skin of his buttocks. This was the steroids. There was nothing but animosity in Control Freak's face when he shot himself up. Then he went on TV as cheerfully as a weather reporter.

I do have to say that it was the discipline I admired. I loved that he lined up his delts and lats to perform these various stunts, that he had forgone endless nights of lusting to arrive there, that he had given up all polite conversation because of the ridicule that would fall on him if he endeavored. I wondered if this were the condition of the fishes that first stepped on land. Were they freakier than bodybuilders? Or were they freakier than we few who have been nailed into coffins?

"This is your spot," he said, pointing to a circle in a square of linoleum on the kitchen floor.

And then the show began. No one except me knew that Control Freak was dressed in nothing but a black posing strap. The audience in their living rooms saw only his face, hypnotizing in its definiteness. It was a face, and a voice, that knew no deviation from a direction. His subject on that day, as it had been on the several afternoons before I was eventually exiled from the home of Sir Edward the M.D., was the force at the bottom of the universe. It was this subject that had totally hooked me and had brought me into the service of Control Freak. I felt that he truly had somewhere to lead me. I kept copious notes during his lectures as I sat naked on a round straw mat on the linoleum floor with only a pad and pencil in my numb hands.

"Religions have always been about control," he said that afternoon, as accurately as I can recall his speech, which I tried to memorize as he spoke.

"The first item they seize control of is the calendar. The calendar was at the center of Mayan religions of human sacrifice. The Christians tried to gain the center of suspense from the Jews by renaming the dates. And the Moslems started the dating all over again. If you control time, you control mind. When you've bracketed the hours from nine to five for working hours, with an hour lunch break, and the two hours afterward as a happy hour for ordering cocktails, then you are in control of the population. You have them by the balls. His or hers."

That was the sociological, global part of his speech. He liked to begin by clueing everybody into what was really going on in the larger world. It was as if he were reading the newspaper to them. Or rereading the newspaper as he rewrote its messages in his own mind. Many times I'd observed Control Freak sitting at his computer, clicking on *The New York Times* home page or *The Washington Post* home page or the MTV home page, searching for current news of great import. Then he'd curse at the screen, disagreeing with the slant with which the news was being reported.

Control Freak's favorite page on the World Wide Web was that of a community led by Frederick of Flagstaff, who had been channeling texts from an angelic intelligence in another sphere now for nine years. The manuscripts were largely prophecies all converging toward a point in the year 2000 or 2001 (depending on various inscrutable computations) during which time the community of his believers, or "controlees," as Control Freak referred to them, would be led onto spaceships to experience the Rapture by escaping through the outer ionosphere of a rapidly unraveling Earth as bombs defaced its pretty blue-and-green complexion with horrors of mutation and cries, "No, he can't die, he can't die, Lord have mercy!" It would be an awful time. I felt it in my gut. But that wasn't what interested Control Freak. He loved the way various fine points of their prophecies would influence their news reporting in special directions. They expected that Israel would cause a nuclear holocaust in which the United States would somehow be pitched against China. So any news of China, or Israel, was always smugly reported if there was any hint of a tilt toward aggression involving any of the three parties. Also there was lots of meteorology: end of world predicted by tidal waves. Their news was at least half weather report, but only reports of weather disasters around the globe. It was one disaster movie after another. I was always happy when Control Freak clicked onto Frederick of Flagstaff's Web page because I knew then I was safe from his impossible moods, which he attributed to steroids, but which I was familiar with in so many before him who had never even heard the word *steroids*, and which I knew to be a primitive condition of zombie masters.

"Why don't you show your body on the set?" I had the boldness to ask on one of those endless afternoons with me lying on the cool floor as he sat in front of the hot computer screen.

"Because I know that I have as much control

over my mind and their minds as I do over my body, you klutz," he answered. "I don't want to dilute or confuse that effect."

"I'm sorry, sir," I answered. By now I knew the script that I was destined to read over the decades and perhaps over the centuries until my death.

"I know that God lives in everybody's souls," he continued on that first afternoon that I was privileged enough to be sitting stageside during a broadcast. "So don't ask yourself what is human, what is truth. Ask yourself whose voice this is that's going out to you, whose voice this is that whispers so true. Who is it who came down from above to set your souls ablaze? It's your brother Lust. And what is the antidote to this terrible Lust? It's worship. But only the worship of power will do for you who are already so far gone. The time has passed for compassion and other noble spiritualist enterprises. Things are too bad. This is the best we can hope for. To get down on your knees in front of your TV sets and worship the strength of my mind and to repeat after me, 'I am peculiar inside.' Know that I can plow you over and pour cement on you and walk all over you so that you will be like everybody else, joined finally to all those others from whom you are so congenitally isolated and alienated. I'm making myself available for your worship. How many others can you find who would say such a thing? In India there are lots. In America and Europe they're few and far between."

Sometimes I have to admit I got exhausted. I just wanted to scream. I lay there aching. He was just going on and on. What if I couldn't stand it anymore? Something inside me got up and wanted to run away. He seemed to sense those moments and grabbed me by the throat, looking at me with those stupid, reptilian eyes. You know that alligators are vividly fast. So if you're in the Everglades and you see an alligator, you can know that the alligator just by being within your purview will be able to reach you and eviscerate you with his teeth in a flash. Once you've seen the green thing it's already too late. That was the speed with which Control Freak would hunt me down, even if he was in the middle of taping one of his sacred shows. Wham! He had me. Wham! He'd wrestled me down. This is sick, I'd be thinking. This is sick. And then I wouldn't be thinking. And then I wouldn't be sick.

Once I started to try to crawl away. I was so overcome by everything. He didn't inject me with any starry powder. Sir Edward the M.D. had been smart to keep me always medicated. Now with the medicine beginning to wear off, for a spell I just wanted to crawl away. It was the shock of oxygen entering the lungs again for the first time. Every so often the entire existence of being a zombie began to feel as if it were a spell about to pass. I passed among the furniture to the outposts of the pots just before the door. Over the Persian rug. I was seeing landscape I didn't usually see. And then he was on me. He knew exactly what I was trying to do. He clenched his hand on the back of my neck and smashed my forehead into the wooden floor. They were all the same, these guys. He began to roar with fury. It was a dream of abuse come true. Who would want such a thing? And why? I had no answers to these questions I was asking myself as I was pounded further and further into it.

Okay. I had to recoup. I had gone too far now to go back, obviously. My legs were weak and rubbery. This was becoming a big drag. But he was dragging me back. He had the kind of muscularity that it was easy for him to overpower me and simply pull me back the way you pull a dog back who's barking at a stranger at the door. So I knew that I had to give in again. I took big, beautiful breaths, gulping down the oxygen at first. I was breathing the way I'd first breathed when I put the air hose in my mouth while scuba-diving. Fear made me suck in the oxygen. It was like overeating to avoid starving. Now I was overbreathing again in a pinch of stress. I imagined the air was blue and filled with glistening white stars that I was swallowing down my throat. Breathing calmed me. I had always felt that so many gestures that regular humans made on the couch with each other, the gulping and sucking on breasts or whatever, were really that they were trying to catch their breath, to gulp down air.

I crawled easily behind Control Freak the rest of the way.

I was back. It had stopped, the nervous doubting. I was submissive again and sort of happy to be so.

"Now it's time for you to start your spiritual training," Control Freak said expansively, full of himself as he usually was around me. "It's the worship of me. It will take away any lingering doubts you still have."

"Uh . . . okay," I said hesitantly.

"So. Use your imagination."

I couldn't believe Control Freak said that.

Yet somehow I knew instinctively what to do. He had set me free to be even more dedicated and monotonous than ever. That was because he knew that by delving into files that had been loaded into my system that first day at the museum unbeknownst to me, I was capable of lots of passive invention. It was simply as if I were taking dictation. This is what the dictation told me to do:

I became like a haircutter. I took a swivel chair and placed it among spotlights and mirrors. In the far corner I placed the TV set filled with dumb daytime soap operas for Control Freak. He loved watching them. "Pop culture is the Hinduism of our time, very polytheistic," he lectured me. He was as usual in his flannel shirt and short blue jean shorts. I thought his muscles were so wild. They were sort of Roman and Greek sculptural. But obviously those guys were swimmers. My brain started to quiver. I fell down at the FILA sneakers of my beloved and began to speak in tongues.

THE BUILDING OF THE ALTAR. It's hard for me to describe. Much more "emotional"—is that the word?—than my usual daily activities. It took days. I pounded the nails into the platform. The wood was piled in a bin down the hall. Apparently an artist lived there. On the platform I put a schoolteacher's chair where Control Freak could sit. Mirrors behind, on side walls, and across from him. Then I built a stepped structure coming down from the main stage. On this ledge I put his favorite objects. I put there his little pocket mirror, a pair of black posing trunks, a medallion won at a contest, a videotape of his own posing. I had the creepy crawlies in my stomach the whole time.

Okay. So he got on the chair. I did get down on the floor. I wasn't exactly kneeling. I was more slumped. "Get on your knees," he said correctively. So I did. I was very good with him. I let the light shine from my eyes. It wasn't the light of intelligence. It was a spotlight sort of light that zombies are gifted with. You can see it in their eyes in almost every movie.

"Now pray to me," he commanded in his biggest voice.

"Okay," I answered in my flattest.

This is what I said: "You make things impossible for everybody, O Great One! . . . Look at you!"

I knew when I was speaking that I was failing.
I knew as I was failing that I was speaking. I knew I
was in trouble. The altar I had built so devotedly, if
shabbily, was beginning to shake. The anger coming
from Control Freak was palpable even without the
breaking of the lumber.

"You don't know anything about worship! . . .
Arrrgh."

By now he was thundering past me on the floor.
He had abandoned the altar after hacking it apart with
his arms and with a nearby ax from over the fireplace.
I didn't know how this would ever work out.

Just when the darkness seemed uncuttable,
final, terminal, Control Freak underwent a mood
swing. He squatted on the corner of the wreckage of
the platform.

To get my attention, Control Freak liked to
smack me in my most sensitive areas, my gonads. He
was doing this repeatedly to draw me into his agenda.
He succeeded on the third whack. I felt as if I had an
instant hernia. Was he going to sell me down the
river just yet?

"Zombie," he whispered, almost encouragingly,
almost romantically, into my hopeless ear.

It was love. I do have a soul! I have a soul of
love! How many times must I say it?

"Zombie, you're not ready for me yet."

Oh no! I started to quiver with seizures of aban-
donment. First my dad! Then Sir Edward the M.D.!

But my fears soon turned out to have been unwarranted. He, the Control Freak, had more to say on the subject.

"You can't run the marathon before you've leaped a single hurdle," he said with great conviction and credibility. "Therefore, Zombie, I'm going to take you to your first religious experience to get your feet wet. From there perhaps you might be able someday to graduate to a deity such as myself."

"And who might that be, master?" I asked politely and, I admit, hopefully. Grace was in the air of the close room.

"That might be the Jesus Men," said Control Freak. "When I'm not worshiping myself, I worship with them."

"Is that true?" I asked naively.

"Yes," he answered me securely.

Oh, what fun. What could be more fun than group worship? But Control Freak was right. I was beginning to fill with a dangerous amount of helium. I would need to be deflated and punctured and bled soon. For my own good. I knew that.

Chapter 11

How Zombie worshiped with the Jesus Men.

CONTROL FREAK BOOKED ON a nonreserved Amtrak train to Washington, D.C., where the Jesus Men were to hold their worship service for fifty-five thousand men at RFK stadium. He wore his beautiful floral pants, and yellow T, and FILA sneakers. Of course I couldn't help but cast back in my mind to WSeal64735. He had been a sweet moment in my young life, perhaps my only true friend. I felt angry at Sir Edward the M.D. for killing him. But what was I to do? Nothing I do seems to matter.

Control Freak pointed to a chair for me to occupy across the aisle from him while he immediately slumped down in his seat and plugged his yellow Walkman earphones into his big ears. He looked so blissful as he crumpled himself into different positions while the train moved past endless examples of everyday life. It was quite a change to be burrowing further and further into a widening hole instead of being imprisoned among four square walls. This novelty kept me occupied for one long quiet stretch of time.

Then the melancholy descended.

I began to feel that I missed other zombies. Perhaps we might be able to seat ourselves in a circle and begin to speak wisely. It's not that zombies are dumb. They're dumb only in relation to other kinds of dumb or smart. But like every creature, they have their own wisdom. I longed to link up with others of my kind and find some solace in our togetherness. Even worms need to be together to tingle from top to bottom. So I too needed to feel that I wasn't entirely alone in this world. Soon enough that stirring would lead me to seek and to find. And then to lose, of course. But that's later.

Eventually Control Freak and I arrived at the beautifully colonnaded train station in Washington, D.C. I found myself dressed for daytime as if I were going on safari in my khaki shorts. I told you about Control Freak's appearance already. I toted a big duffel bag filled with his stuff, which we dropped at a hotel. (Shades of going scuba-diving with Sir Edward the M.D.!) Then we moved toward the horizon dominated by a blue sky. We took a taxi driven by a Somalian cabdriver who had lots to say about our upcoming experience.

"What's going on at RFK?" he asked.

"The Jesus Men," Control Freak answered gruffly.

"What's that?" he asked, though I could anticipate his question from a million miles away, even me.

"Christian men, many of them athletes, who get together in stadiums to worship Christ and reaffirm their promises to God, country, wife, and family," Control Freak explained.

"What do they think about Jesus?" the cabdriver asked.

"What do you mean?" Control Freak answered noncommittally.

"Do they think he's going to return?"

"Yes, eventually."

"I'm a Muslim. But from Somalia. We believe that Jesus is a prophet, like Moses or Mohammed. But we believe that Jesus is going to return to preach at the end of time. No man knows if it will be now or later. We don't believe that Jesus was crucified. We believe that he survived the cross and was just taken directly up into heaven later."

"Well, that's a sect of Islam, then; it's certainly not the center mainstream ideology doctrine," said Control Freak learnedly as he pushed his FILAs up against the back of the seat to express his irritation.

"Don't get too wrapped up in it," the cabdriver warned. "Sometimes people who get into religion go crazy."

"Ho, ho, ho," Control Freak laughed. I knew he was being dismissive. The cabdriver, however, may have misinterpreted his response as being somehow jovial.

Although I knew that Islam Men and Jesus Men

were rivals on different teams, I also knew from shows I'd watched on the educational program that Islam Men gathered together also shoulder to shoulder, rank on rank, submitting themselves to a greater power, a power that could impel them to work and think and bow as one, that demanded respect and total, complete, and fundamental allegiance.

Our arrival in the stadium was thrilling. Outside the actual concrete shell of the stadium many colorful tents were set up where vendors were selling their wares. It was very spiritual and beautiful. When I had wandered the streets of New York City on those rare afternoons when I wasn't chained up or otherwise employed in doing chores for Control Freak, I had reveled in visiting the religious novelty stores. I felt particularly drawn to the colorfully painted statues of Mary, the mother of God, of Jesus in his blue robes as if he were clothed in the sky and the clouds, as well as to the metal crosses on which his dead body was strung and then spray-painted in glorious golds or silvers. I worshiped among the trinkets and rosaries and medallions of saints who were, I suppose, the celebrities of their time. Well, here they were selling their beautiful all-male hymn singing on CDs and cassettes. They were offering hats, sweatshirts, T-shirts, mugs. A T-shirt I particularly admired on a young surfer who passed by bore the legend "His Pain, My Gain." The graphic was a bloody hand through which a nail had been pounded, causing drops of crimson blood that stood out in highlights against the white background of the T-shirt. Another bore the inscription "A Man Who Is Reborn Is Born a New Man." I understood the concept of birth through death quite well. Suddenly I felt at home.

The atmosphere on the ground was electric. The heavens were about to drop on all of us. But the skies were hesitating, mixing their messages. The men were practically bursting their jeans with anticipation. Boys, men, fathers, sons, church members, brothers. You could almost smell the DNA cooking. We walked among the multitudes. Many were tossing implements to one another: footballs, Frisbees, paper airplanes, lime green tennis balls, blown-up pastel balloons. We found our folding metal seats in the orchestra section, which was located on the playing field itself.

"I have seats on the fifty-yard line," one worshiper bragged as we passed by.

"That's sweet," his friend replied.

Then the music began! A live orchestra was located onstage beneath an electronic scoreboard on which was etched a cross. There were cymbals, drums, saxes, an electronic keyboard, an organ. The stadium was filled with the exaltation of bass chords. The men went wilder and wilder, circulating as the wave, a maneuver from football games and rock concerts in which everyone would rise with their arms shoved above their heads like riders on a roller coaster. This introduction led into a series of rugged hymns that seemed well suited to the surround of men. "Holy! Holy! Holy!" they sang with all the fullness of their lungs and their guts, transposing religion into a baritone key. I stood proudly next to Control Freak as the shivers spread contagiously among the men. Soon they were holding one arm, or both arms, up, exaltingly, feeling the spirit, making a spiritual touchdown. I began to cry, first in little whimpers, then in exchanges with myself that were unexplainable. How could these waves be washing over me? Who am I to feel anything? It was "Holy! Holy! Holy!" And then it was "All Hail the Power of Jesus' Name!" And then it was "How Great Thou Art!"

I was taken back thanks to the acrid spray of the perfume of my memories to my earliest days in my Pennsylvania town. That is where I first experienced religion. Sure, there was the spiritual moment in the museum that changed everything forever. Why did I want to lurk in a dusty museum when other children wanted to play in the sun? I asked myself then, and I ask myself now. But I also had plenty of experiences with my kin in the family of Christianity. Once I had been thrown to my knees by a vision of a flame above my four-poster walnut bed. The flame talked. It was Moses! That was something. Another time, lying in that same bed, my body a stiff nail, I heard the words *Look up to heaven!* That was something, too. The most electrifying moment was when I attended a showing of the movie *The Cross and the Switchblade* in my high school auditorium. It was sponsored by an evangelist who wasn't there but who had sent his deputies to convert us for him. Well, it worked for me. Pat Boone starred. Billy Graham lent his name. The film traded on constant hints of violence, switchblades, leather jackets. Soon after the words *The End* rolled down the sliding expanse of the screen, they asked us to come forward. Wow! I'm not sure why I did except that I felt so emotional and spiritual and excited by all the violence and darkness depicted in the movie. I felt the film was somehow speaking my language. I came forward to commit my life to Jesus. Jesus was certainly true and beautiful. He never said anything wrong so far as I could tell. He seemed pure to me. And so did the dark violence of the film. When they let us go—we who had humbled ourselves by coming forward in this tacky auditorium—I sneaked a stretched touch at the silver movie screen gone dead just a foot or so away. The hit man of the absent evangelist gave me a dirty look, but I didn't care. I knew I had felt the spirit that evening.

The Jesus Men service came to its crescendo when Franklin Graham, the son of Billy Graham, spoke to the gathered basses and baritones. I found significance in his father's having been so crucial in my own spiritual development. As he began to speak, an entire downpour of pins of rainwater pierced the skin of all of us present. Control Freak dug it. He lay back in his chair and practically basked in the needling shower. He showed that he was truly aligned with the spirit as Speaker Graham outlined the matter at hand. He told all the men present that if they ran for cover, they were "wimps." That Jesus had suffered untold discomforts to save their souls from the damnation of eternal hell. Speaker Graham came across as a real man. I don't remember much of what he said. Okay, I don't remember anything of what he said. But he was dressed in blue jeans and a green-and-white-striped Jesus Men polo shirt. I think he even had on brown cowboy boots. His voice was deep, like that of the lead singer in a musical comedy with an "original soundtrack album" my parents used to play in Pennsylvania, before I was thrown out of earshot of the syrupy thing. At the end many men came forward, though perhaps not as many as he wished. It was like an election. How many men could you get to vote for God? As the boys came forward, others slapped them on the backs of their shoulders to egg them on. I did not come forward. Neither did Control Freak.

"I can worship the one true living God," he explained to me kindly. "But that doesn't mean I have to kiss His feet!"

I understood his problem with the whole thing. I mean, everybody had their own problems with such

excesses, I guess. I missed some of the more demand-
ing exhibitions of commitment and three-dimensional
compliance: bloodletting or branding, for instance.

The ride home on the metro system of Washington, D.C., was lovely. As we stood perplexed before
the machines that would map out our route, some of
the believers offered us dollar bills if we needed them
for the machine that sucked them up, or quarters for
its extra piece of equipment designed to swallow
quarters. If the dollar-bill acceptor was a mouth, the
quarter acceptors were ears. The men were very free
with information. It was as if they had learned man-
ners in the stadium. What could be better? Control
Freak was equally placid. He gentlemanly allowed
me to sit first, before him, on the double seat. When
it looked as if a black man might be needing the seat
opposite us, he lifted his newspaper to make room
for him.

Needless to say, his behavior in our room on a
traffic circle in a hotel made of cardboard was not
nearly so lovely and acceptable. He seemed to feel
the need to balance his stadium etiquette with an
equal amount of abusiveness and actually certifiable
madness and unacceptable bellicosity. "Take this,"
were his only words the entire night. It is finished, I
thought. The hit was to the side of my head. It was
direct, blow by blow. The blood and the gashes and
stitches were inseparable. The roving hand was
imminent but never recognized, always a surprise

and an affront to any construction of personality possible. Was this the end? When the house doctor came and sewed up one side of my head with little red stitches, a dozen or so, I felt that this was evidence admissible in a trial. But of course it wasn't. It was actually a cover-up. We both managed a few hours of sleep that night. And then it was time to worship again. None of the other sixty thousand men in the stadium seemed to notice my stitches, which had not been there the night before.

There were a number of fantastic moments that day. The first, and perhaps the finest, was the return of the youths. The administrators sent all the sons out of the stadium for a few hours, which seemed like years, while a speaker instructed the men on how exactly to love their wives. I found this segment of the show a bit dry because the wives weren't there to soak it up as well. It was like talking about them while they were out of the room. But when the boys returned, six thousand of them in all, they ran in lifting little white crosses over their heads. Their fathers stood up and cheered them on. A leader told with crackling voice how he had grown up fatherless. "We love you, son!" the fathers were chanting. The boys were saluting wildly with their little crosses. Promises were made to adopt boys without fathers. The men were crying. The boys were puffing up their chests proudly, not understanding anything except the emotion of the moment. That's when I joined in.

I remembered disconsolately the rifts between my own father and me, which came to a head at the bus station. It must have been tough to have a zombie for a son. I understood where he was coming from. But at the same time I minded the trouble that it bred.

"Let's get a hot dog, Zombie," Control Freak said to me softly with, I imagined, a certain tenderness in his voice.

"Sure," I whispered hopefully.

The trip to the snack bar was a moment of healing in my own crisis of being somehow male, though more significantly zombie. Control Freak bought me everything in sight. We climbed to a high balcony to consume it all, sitting among a church of men who were all dressed in lime green baseball caps. A decorated officer onstage talked ramblingly about his experiences as a marine in Vietnam, a particularly God-soaked place according to him. But I must admit that I was too absorbed in the free food to notice. I loved the soft pretzels covered in a goo of yellow mustard. I'd swallowed by mistake a hot dog that popped into my throat like an umber balloon. Then the pizza in a square box, so puffed with starchiness I imagined I'd swallowed a bed covered in cheese on which someone had bled. Tall Cokes, one after another, followed. I soon felt entirely drugged with a whirring, disorienting bunch of reactions.

"Thank you for the burritos," was all I could say to Control Freak at that heightened moment, but

I felt so much more. I felt that thanks was a fountain of blood bursting from my heart through my chest in extraordinary pulsings, as in a horror show. Nothing crucifies and cuts like ecstatic joy!

The rest of the day meandered in slow rivulets from the emotional peak of eating snacks with Control Freak. I felt as if he were truly the replacement for WSeal64735.

"Don't try to be clever," Control Freak said to me as he brushed my hand away from his cropped, wiry locks.

"Oh," I replied, practically with a burp.

Much of the remainder of the afternoon schedule was taken up with a special plea for reconciliation of black men with white men, referred to as "breaking down the walls." I, however, in my special condition, had never considered the difference of skin shade to be much of a difference. I knew the difference between truly human people and zombies. That's how I divided the world. So I found that message a bit flat. Still, the sun did come out for the last hour. After all the rain, that was a curtain-raiser. Mostly I sat staring at Control Freak. It was a wonderful opportunity to do so, as this racial issue mollified and absorbed him for the entire time. He didn't know I was alive. I mean, he didn't know it even more so than he usually didn't know it.

Control Freak happened to be dressed the same way he was the first day I was lucky enough to meet him. His plaid cotton shirt was opened onto his torso, his cutoffs coarse in the sharpening sun, revealing his legs like trunks. I thought that the determination he exhibited was some sort of a culmination. A spiritual message was the firecracker. "Let us pray," they said. And I did. I did. But I was really praying to Control Freak because he was really there. I guess that's finally what made me a zombie rather than a human. And what made me turn finally, reluctantly, away that afternoon from this religion, no matter how delicious its hot dogs or how heart puncturing its father-and-son psychology.

Indeed, that's how they left it. It was a passage read, and videographed, about the Father showing up at the baptism of His son, Jesus Christ, and being well pleased. What a great dad, I thought. But I knew He wasn't my dad. My dad put me on the bus.

Chapter 12
Control Freak's gift.

I N THE WEEKS FOLLOWING our peak experience at the Jesus Men rally, we resumed our old routines. The beatings. The new additions to the altar: a column on which I'd tacked towels discarded on the bathroom floor by Control Freak; garlands wrapped around the base of the platform where he sat while I pointed out and praised nuanced changes in his every muscle. By now Control Freak was shooting up with steroids pretty regularly, so his moods were subject to quick rises and falls, not unlike Sir Edward the M.D. with his ostensibly quite different medicine cabinet. Hah!

One afternoon Control Freak revealed to me again that he was getting a little bored with my forms of worship. I started to worry severely when he said that. I felt prickles of sweat break out on my forehead and back, the pitter-pattering of my heart, the tears filling the drain of my throat. I began to discover that I was not the only one in Control Freak's life. He had obviously tired of me somewhat. He was beginning to attract a continuous line of visitors, both male and female, who would show up from late morning until late evening. The arbitrary timing of their endless visits would have been of no consequence to me. The bad part I'm getting to is that Control Freak didn't really want me around when the others, whoever they were, visited. Even though I was supposedly living in the loft, I was spending much of my time in the cold. It was winter, and the trees had turned into skeletons. I worried while I rounded the block hundreds of thousands of times.

"I think you should commit to a certain number of hours every day when you serve me, your living god," Control Freak said one afternoon as he stood, obviously listless and bored, next to his washing machine with his cell phone. I knew that what he was referring to in a pinpoint was the doing of the laundry.

I, of course, readily agreed to this curlicue in our contract. But what was to happen during the rest of the hours?

What happened was that I was practically homeless in New York City. I was indentured to a person whose ego knew no bottom and no top. Which was practically the definition of a god. But the constant feeding, the constant sacrifice, would have been quite impossible for even the most emptied of beings. Control Freak possessed an infinite capacity for the worship of himself, and a desire as well for novelty, for new tastes to be offered up as sacrifices.

He was as brutal as an Aztec in his appetites. All my travels had only helped me to further define and understand his true nature.

In the meantime I took to the streets. I ate beautiful hot dogs at Nathan's shop on Times Square. The mustard was as sleek and slippery as an oil slick catching the golden sheen of a setting sun. I murmured along Eighth Avenue, where everyone seemed a close cousin to me, they behaved in such a disoriented way. That is, they possessed an attention span that went endlessly from left to right with no differentiation that would allow them to be distracted, though they were filled with a kind of sexual percolation foreign and much too self-centered for me, and probably for other truly dead souls as well. I was beginning to be particularly concerned with who and what I was exactly, and how closely their tastes matched up with me and with mine. I was being hurled unintentionally by Control Freak into an identity crisis. It was as if I were dialing a number repeatedly where nobody answered and to which there was no answering machine attached.

This waiting trained me. I could have used the opportunity to visit the great museums and multiplexes of the city. But the deal was that Control Freak would call me whenever he desired me to report back to what had briefly been my home base and from which I was gradually being dispatched. The checkpoint was the very phone booth at which I had initially contacted Control Freak a season or so ago.

"I think you'd be better off if you were dead," Control Freak said rudely to me one evening when we were blissfully alone. I knew things were reaching a climax of unpleasantness. I'd been through this so many times before in my search.

"You may worship me one last time," he added as if it were an afterthought rather than a climactic, earth-rumbling statement. "I've met a woman who will become my wife. But to cut the embarrassment you must be feeling, that envelope over there contains a gift for you."

I felt crumpled. I remembered all the hours in my high school classes I'd spent staring into the drum of the gray metal trash can situated near my seat in homeroom. I felt again consigned to that gloomy, resonant space that was so other. It was like being vacuumed up into an empty pipeway. All my insides were somehow outside me, and only the outside was in. I kept returning over and over again to this spot. It seemed to be the ground on which I walked and on which I would be eventually buried. This feeling was my funeral plot.

But not entirely. For I was transfixed by the lovely light green envelope that lay on the table, practically glowing. It was a long business envelope. Not a big thing or a small boxy square thing. Its lime green was special. It was the green I'd seen on caterpillars, on snow peas as they tumbled out of the zipper of their pods. It was the green of Control Freak's snot, which made it particularly evocative for me. It was the green of the pond of the Japanese gardens of the Brooklyn Botanic Gardens, where I had walked one day, five hours in each direction. It was the green of clover that I used to spend entire months of my boyhood looking for, hunting and pecking out of the other varieties of weeds. I wondered what was in the envelope. I knew, though, that that was for later, the last thing. For now we were in the moment of the next to the last thing.

I savored an unusual sort of worship that evening. Not at all like the other worship sessions we'd enjoyed in months gone by. Control Freak was dressed the way he was the first time I was granted an audience with him during the previous winter. His garb provided a magical closure: you know, the open plaid shirt, the tight shorty-short blue jeans with belt. Everything else, though, was quite different. For starters, Control Freak was snorting coke. I knew what it was from Sir Edward the M.D. and his steady diet of white powder and cabbage soup. But I had never known Control Freak to indulge. Tiny snowflakes fell and stuck on the soft flesh of his top lip. He continued snorting as if he had the sniffles.

"I'm gonna be high while you worship me, I hope you don't mind," he said irrelevantly, addressing the snidely polite comment to the blaring, silver glowing window rather than to me. "Do you like Special K?"

I wore a bright red dog collar. I was stripped of all of my clothes except a tight black leather corset with snaps on both sides that I wore tightly. Control Freak stripped down to just his white briefs and construction boots with white socks. He became engaged with the far wall, made entirely of mirroring glass. He liked to hang from the doorway jamb like an ape to stare at himself as he stretched there. I commented favorably on his lats, on the complete absence of body fat he exhibited as he posed in the flattering doorway. By now I was flat on the floor on my stomach, looking up sweetly with my chin propped on my hands. It was bittersweet to be worshiping him from whom I was so soon to be so poignantly separated.

Control Freak took me into the bathroom. We'd never been in the bathroom together. "I'm gonna give you an enema," he said quite directly.

And he did. The bathroom was made entirely of black tiles. Control Freak's different creams and pills and supplements and hairsprays and sprawling toiletries kits took up the entire surface of a rather extensive marbleized sink area. "Lie down in the tub on your stomach," he continued. Given the context and the goings-on, the revelry was taking on more of the sentimental trappings of a bachelor's party than a worship service. "Did you call me 'white trash'?" he asked loudly and inexplicably.

"What do you mean?" I responded weakly.

"All the trash is in your white behind," he

answered mysteriously. By then I was lying in the tub on my stomach. He inserted into my behind the nozzle of a silver device, turning on a hose of water that began to fill my stomach so that I was soon the proud mother of a water balloon. He liked to press me down as he did, my stomach barely flattening against the curve of the tub. In the olden days he might have cracked my head against the porcelain. I would have understood that. But this form of attention was so weirdly fleshy, I was unaccustomed. It almost implied I had a body as he had a body. What was he doing to me? Raising me up?

"Squat on the toilet," he commanded. The seat was cranked up, so I simply allowed myself to flutter down onto a bare rim. "Empty yourself," he said as he settled to watch from a chair in the far room, looking at me as if through the wrong end of a telescope. I began losing my circumference, understanding then and there how women felt who lost babies. Those women were strapped to so many rugged crosses on Calvary. I understood loss, and the sensuality of loss. Because so much of life is about loss. I mean, I was losing Control Freak, as well as a baby of pure water.

"You look beautiful there," he said from the vantage point of the wooden schoolteacher's chair on which he was sprawled. "You know how vulnerable it is to be where you are doing what you're doing naked?"

Well, "No" was the actual answer, but I didn't use

that answer. I just shut up and went about my business. I knew I was just an isthmus to him at that moment. Not a continent. Or a landmass. How had he undergone this transition? I didn't know the answer, of course, and he wasn't about to supply it, of course.

Then came the sequence in Control Freak's bedroom. I spent the first part of those several hours in his shoe closet. He had the most exciting, varied collection of shoes imaginable. I practically swallowed a pair of thongs in my mouth whole. There was a pair of white sneakers as bright as Pepsodent. Beautiful, classic, black-tie shoes. Somehow I made my way to a clearing on the floor. He was on the bed, talking on the phone, quite oblivious of my meandering, roaming the phone sex lines and writing down numbers to call. I couldn't discern if he was talking to girls or guys. It was all the same. He described my douched behind et cetera. As I've said, the wall was mirrors. He was in a glory of coke sniffing. All was very dicey and impure, but somehow innocent and foursquare, too. Only gods can carry off that kind of dichotomous success.

"Your tongue tasted very good on my arm," he said to me the next morning. I must confess I didn't recall such a moment. He might have been speaking figuratively.

What I do recall as vividly as lightning was the light green envelope! I actually slept in the same bed as Control Freak that evening. I don't remember how it happened. I curled at the bottom of the expansive bed he allowed himself. His feet were clothed in white socks. He woke up with a start. "You wanna shower or you just wanna split?" he asked in an unclear voice. I divined that he wanted me to leave without the shower. So I quickly scrambled for my mound of clothes and put them on. "There it is," he said, pointing toward the envelope. I opened the thing and at first couldn't make out its implications. It looked like a bus ticket. Was he sending me back to Pennsylvania? But no. Far different. "It's a one-way ticket to Port-au-Prince," he explained.

"What's Port-au-Prince?" I asked reasonably.

"It's the capital of Haiti." Stuck in along with the ticket was a clean green hundred-dollar bill and a fake passport with my own blurred image glued in. Oh no! Could anything have been more kind! Here was a partial-expense-paid one-way vacation.

As I slunk past the unpacked cartons that made up most of his home, and with whose potential I'd been living now for months, I felt nothing but zapped. Control Freak had understood me. I was amazed that he'd chosen a destination so seared in my little head since that first exhibition at the Scranton museum that kept whispering about Haiti, Haiti, Haiti. Sure, my head was bowed as I walked out through pedestrians who knew nothing of my pain and sorrow. But I walked knowing that what I had of a heart had truly been pierced. And that was truly something I owed entirely to Control Freak.

Chapter 13

How Zombie addresses his loneliness by going on a spiritual quest to the island of Hispaniola.

YOU CAN'T IMAGINE HOW floored I was landing on Haiti. I'd never been outside the states of Pennsylvania, Ohio, and New York. I was like one of those agoraphobic people I'd seen finally lured onto a talk show for a few hundred dollars. They'd spent fifteen years in front of their TVs afraid to face a bigger, threatening world of traffic lights, car washes, magazine stands, underwear shops, tanning parlors. And understandably so. Here I was transported within three extremely uncomfortable hours—imagine three hours stuck in an elevator with the same people. Transported to a Caribbean island!

It's hard to explain the transition I was going through. It was like walking down a piano's keyboard made of black and white keys in search of a chord, or even a dischord, that matched the resonance of my own heart. It was like being on a disconnected methedrine trip. How was I ever to find the key to my own heartless heart? I mean, I was and am a monster droning on. Luckily I was first hit by the topography, which was so other that I was immediately subsumed in my own longing and desire and belonginglessness so that I was at least able to see. I've found that the clearer the windshield, the more uncomfortable the drive!

I landed at the airport of Port-au-Prince. Can you imagine? The main hangar of the airport where passengers loaded and disembarked was a slanted sailor's cap. It had no dignity. It had merely a slant. But even I was sure that in the international Esperanto of airports the language of the airport was meant to speak loudly of the country. How those words pumped themselves into my head! Maybe I was already in Haiti! I mean, I was already in Haiti! According to the travel book I found in economy class on the airplane, the mountains were going to stretch up into the sky.

I want to report on Haiti. I truly do. I mean, it's another country. But I can't. Because everything's become all the same. Anyway, I went immediately to a hotel for which I could make out the markings in my Michelin Guide. I couldn't believe Control Freak had provided such a cantilever to me. I was there during the rainy season of early spring, so most of the time I was drenched by sudden downpours.

Port-au-Prince is an exotic town. Certainly there were none of the skyscrapers that had impressed me so devastatingly on my arrival in New York City. But what it lacked in buildings it made up for in these mountains that were like the skeletons of giant dinosaurs left stranded by an indifferent sea. Steep mountains towered over the city from nearby Gonave Island, which lay in a horseshoe bay on the west, and another wall of mountains beyond a rift valley plain to the left. I was staying in a villa whose name I forget in a quiet neighborhood at the top of avenue John Paul II, a ten-minute walk from the nearest taxi stand. It had one generator, so the room lights came on with power only about nine o'clock for an hour or so. They had generously provided a fan in the room. When the lights went on, I could lie on the floor in front of the fan in my shorts to feel the electrically generated tropical breezes. Being on the floor in such a faraway spot reminded me of my tropical vacation with Sir Edward the M.D. Remember that cadaver? Otherwise there were no tropical breezes. But often there were long electrical blackouts for days. When the electricity went, so did the heavily rationed water. Hot bottled guava juice was my favorite local delicacy.

During my first week I took walks. My favorite destinations were the shantytowns they called "bidonvilles" thriving along marshy waterfronts to the north of the center of the city. Garbage was rarely collected, so enormous mounds were stinking up the streets. But the locals didn't seem unduly rancorous because of this. Unless you found them sticking a hand into the pockets of your shorts to discover, well, in my case very little—a loose cigarette, a few *gourdes*, which were the local unit of currency. The guidebook was a big help. I visited out of respect the white, triple-domed presidential palace. I had never been to the White House, so this seemed a chance to make up for my lack of closeness to centers of power of that sort. I always loved people of power. A tour guide gave us the scoop in English: "It was built on the site of a predecessor that was blown up in 1912 with its president inside." I love nothing better than going on tours. On this tour the guide pointed out to us the very bullet holes in the walls shot there during the 1991 coup to make the palace guard surrender while President Aristide was making a stand inside. I felt those tiny contusions with my very own hands. Then I passed through a burned-out, irregularly shaped park called the Champs de Mars (perhaps because of its scorched pink grass) to visit the teeming commercial quarter that my guide-book said "lacks charm or interest . . . is now very run down." I, however, bought a lovely boxed kaleidoscope there with which I spent many delightful hours.

But enough postcards! Not that there weren't many fine ones to send back home. (If I had a home, that is.) Complete strangers of different shades of black, brown, and white offered me coffee or cola. A row of terrace cafés sold barbecued chicken at the southeast corner of the Champs de Mars, starting near the Rex theater. At the city's western limits, around Mariani, at an ill-lit waterfront club, Le Lambi, couples danced groin to groin to live hypnotic voodoo drumming bands while the men ate plate after plate of spicy, freshly caught conch to boost their vitality in much the same way Control Freak used to pop pills of bright red ginseng. (I did begin to miss him when there were such poignant reminders of his exultations. How sweetly he did display himself!) I loved the television and radio antennas that dotted the tops of the peaks of mountains about the city. The telephones, though, were useless. Remember that frequent power cuts can plunge entire neighborhoods into darkness. Drivers always had to carry a license as police blocks were common at nights. Pssst! Watch out for pickpockets in markets and bus terminal areas and inside buses. Take mosquito repellent.

All of this detail, of course, ignores my mission on the half island of Haiti. That came my way by way of Nancy, actually. Nancy was an ethnopharmacologist from Harvard University. She had silver blond hair styled in the most fetching manner. Her clothes were minimal, usually just a phosphorescent green piece of cloth that wrapped around her extremely worked-out body. What was left to dangle toward the earth tantalizingly were her legs. They were long, identical twins. Nancy was definitely on a trip of the finest variety. I was honored to meet her one day while we were both poking among the hookah devices at the local bazaar, the Woolworth's of the Caribbean. I felt like screaming at her when I met her, but I didn't.

"Who are you?" she asked reasonably enough.

"I'm someone who's been sent as far away as I can possibly imagine in all this dirtiness to find myself," I answered reasonably enough.

"But you're so cute," she responded.

"Can you help me?" I asked hopefully.

"I could be a helper," she answered to the best of her ability. "What can I help you with?"

"I'm a zombie from the U.S.A.," I informed her crisply.

"That's brilliant," she said. She had actually been brought up in London, England, by two Americans on a lifelong lark. "For what are you searching, boy?"

"I'm always searching for my identity through the force field of a director," I confessed. "A mesmerist," I went on. "But now I wonder to myself about my fellow zombies, where they are, who they are, if they exist."

"Of course you do," she said sweetly, sexily, beautifully, as directly as an arrow, and as far outly as a female bodybuilder with biceps and all the gyrations of a gymnast's hips.

"Can you help me?" I repeated even more hopefully.

"Yes," she said. "Yes, I can, amazingly enough. By one of those life-is-stranger-than-fiction coincidences, you're saying just the right thing to just the right person."

"You can?" I continued as if trapped in a routine I couldn't shake out of.

"I'm going to lead you to my Jeep, darling," she said. She was so Hollywood in her intellectual way that she could say or do anything. She could get away with murder. "I'm going to load you in my Jeep and we're going to take a ride, and along the way I'm going to tell you a story, maybe *the* story as far as you're concerned. I just hope I'm not leading you to your own demise."

"I hope so, too," I replied.

Then we were off. I had no idea in which direction the road was going. I enjoyed the dozens of ruined plantation houses, the radio and television masts sticking up in thin air here as they had on the mountains surrounding Port-au-Prince, the town where the locals freely pee on public beaches. At first Nancy tried to be an entertaining tourist guide, telling me of all the bygone disasters whose cherished memories we were bypassing and all the traditional sites.

"This town lost maybe fifteen hundred residents when an overloaded ferryboat, the *Neptune*, sank on the way to Port-au-Prince a few years ago," she said directly into the hot, dry wind that was skimming over the top of the Jeep's visor so that I barely caught her words.

"Columbus anchored here in 1492 two days before his flagship sank."

"There are caves near here inhabited by millions of bats."

"This is Morne Rouge, the sugar plantation that spawned the big voodoo slave revolt when they massacred the French, massacring and torching the French motherfuckers, until they got their way." Nancy was passionate sometimes about politics, it seemed. "The sugar was soaked in red, hence the name of the place, perhaps."

I had a peek for myself at the Saint d'Eau waterfall, after huffing and puffing up a detour of a trail, while Nancy still in the Jeep waited smartly below. This sacred waterfall was overhung by creepers as it fell what looked like three miles down into shallow pools separated by mossy limestone shelves. The falls did seem enchanted. I mean, it wasn't my kind of excitement. But exciting in a nice, normal sort of way. Sure, I could see it, the lugubrious greens full of dark shadows, the hint of a body floating unexposed all the way downstream to its eventual drowning.

"The voodooists bathe themselves in its waters to purify themselves," Nancy told me as she ripped out. "They light candles to enlist the help of the ancient spirits."

By now I'd seen enough phosphorescent green mood patches of falling water to appreciate the subtle joke in the envelope Control Freak had left for me. Haiti had more shades of green than I'd ever seen or dreamed. I was finding that I didn't particularly connect to any of this voodoo lore, though. I felt much more alert when Nancy talked about "rot gut" and the local herbal teas used to combat it. I was beginning to understand that there was some old-fashioned notion of zombies, and lore, and a history, and a civilization. But I felt it had *nothing* to do with me. I knew I had contemporaries. And I felt they were here.

Maybe only because they'd been drawn by the same fake lore, the "hook." Finally Nancy got to it.

"So I started to meet these weird guys," she said, and when she did I heard a new tune emerging.

"I started to meet them here in Haiti," she said, pushing farther down on the pedal that controlled the gas flow. "They were mainly Americans. What they all had in common was a sweet mien."

"Mien?" I asked.

"Face," she explained brusquely.

"Oh, face," I repeated back to her.

"Yes. Each was attractive physically. Each was a male. I have yet to meet a female zombie, although I expect that they are out there and I'm awaiting the day. Each had a desire to serve, or not to serve, exactly, but to bear the weight of the last impression left on them. It was as if they had given up. They were very much like you. Adorable ciphers in need of a ride. And I gave that ride to them. And eventually we kept winding up at the same ranch. Which means that I can take you to that ranch. To meet those boys. And to meet as well their *oungan*."

"What's that?"

"Like a voodoo priest. I think there are as many as three boys I've brought there he's preying on. But it's not the usual bad scene. You'll see. It's a special place for you types to find yourself or something."

"Greeeeat," I said, finally getting the idea. "This, I believe, is why I came. . . . And because I had little choice."

"No choice, sweetheart," Nancy pointed out sweetly.

Screeech. We pulled up in the storm of dust created by her lurching on the stick shift.

The building we pulled up to was a gray ranch house situated in a raggedy grove of trees ripe with poisonous bright red berries. Its shiny plate-glass windows were blocked by the stripes of closed venetian blinds. Out the colonial door with knocker came walking a paramilitary young man. His black hair was cropped short with one of those tails of hair left growing longer down the back. His aviator glasses reflected Nancy and me as we stood against the side of the Jeep, me a few inches shorter than she. He wore a gray T-shirt, the sleeves chopped off, green-and-brown military fatigues, black combat boots. A handmade cigarette hung from one side of his lifeless mouth. His hands were finer that I'd expected at first glance. They were a piano player's hands.

"Nancy, wussus you bring with you thees time?" he said, appraising me in a quick glance, then boring down on her. His voice reminded me of the reruns of Ricky Ricardo in *I Love Lucy* I'd devoured on endless afternoons in the loft of Control Freak.

This was Carlos, I later found out. His nickname, though, which he often preferred to go by, was Raw. Carlos was proud of his ancestry in Puerto Rico, where he'd been raised, where he'd worked the first years of his adult life as a cop, and where he'd learned many of the techniques for either quelling, or inciting, or provoking, or subduing prisoners, techniques used to great success on many of his young zombie captives. He was not your typical *oungan*. apparently. Nor was his sixties pad of a house a typical *ounphor*—the voodoo temple where the priests can usually be located, as Nancy explained.

"Nancy, iss hot outside, why you not come in where the a.c izz?" Carlos asked as he wrapped his arm about her. He was kind of a rat. But a rat with a ratty charisma that I would soon come to worship as if it were the force of night and shadow. When he took off his glasses he had eyes that were hypnotic. Carlos was a cop. So that's it, I realized. He and Nancy were having a thing. I was here as a kind of gift. She wasn't helping me. She was helping herself. It was good to feel used and manipulated again.

"Come in," Nancy said nonchalantly to me as she rubbed against him, and they disappeared into the rectangle of black violet the door had become by being opened. It was the shape, I realized, of a grave.

Carlos snapped his fingers at me the minute I was through the door. Before even my eyes had adjusted. I knew the treatment. By now I was not just temperamentally one of them, I had begun to understand a universal etiquette that derived from who knew where. It might as well have been genetic. "Take off your clothes and seat there," he said, his endearing Spanish accent heavily with him. I did

remove the scraps of Americana I was wearing—
jeans, T-shirt, sneaks. Always the same uniform.
Then I sat down on the wall-to-wall carpet with a
shiver. The a/c was indeed on full blast. He and
Nancy went off to the bedroom for what could have
been hours. They were giggling. I could hear the clat-
ter of glasses or ice. I distinctly heard the rip of teeth
against plastic as a package was opened. I had plenty to occupy me, to help me acclimate. I was home
again. I could feel that. The way that zombies were
first discovered to be real, rather than mythological
figments, Nancy told me, was when visitors to Haiti
would see them in snaking lines like chain gangs,
without, of course, the superfluous leg irons, shuffling down the roads of the farms in their pajamalike
clothes, wearing their dreamlike expressions.

The room I was in was soothing. It was pretty
empty. There were some oversize couches and oversize
burlap chairs. The lights dimmed. A bad velvet paint-
ing of a girl with an orphaned expression hung on the
wall. Where there would normally have been a TV
there was a huge fish tank. The entire time I was waiting, a fat ugly fish with teeth like a can opener was
attacking mercilessly, then tearing apart slowly, then
devouring, this beautiful littler fish with lovely yellow
stripes that I kept thinking was an angelfish for no
good reason. I know nothing about little fish. I know
only about sharks. But from what I'd learned about
sharks, the ugly grouper was behaving similarly to the

infinitely more beautiful tiger shark. Pretty soon the pristine tank—it looked as though it had just been bought—was sullied with the tatters of fish flesh floating through its aquamarine hell.

"I hate TV," were Carlos's first words as he emerged from the bedroom in a paisley bathrobe like some kind of starring boxer, Nancy hanging on his shoulder in panties and an extraneous bra. "You'll never see TV here," he warned. But I was thinking about my mum and my dad at that moment. Sadness does better without television, anyway.

"Let me take you on a cleaning tour," he said. At first I didn't understand what he meant. But clarity came quickly enough.

The cleaning tour was not nearly as grueling as his tone had implied. And it gave me an opportunity to take in the rest of the ranch house before I arrived in the zombic chamber, where I'd be spending most of my days and nights in suspension with my comrades, as if we were ensconced in larvae, or cocoons. Where we would not be allowed to move except on set occasions to talk. "Here isss a scooper," Carlos explained as he handed me a sieve attached to a long stick. "Scoop out thee shit from zee tank. Then change thee salt water with theese hose and theese bucket." Sometimes his accent was pronounced, sometimes entirely absent. I set to work.

The room was beautiful. Its floor—and the flooring of every room in the house—was covered with thick gray carpeting. One wall was taken up almost entirely with the aquarium, bubbling and gasping all for the benefit of one killer grouper. Some plaster-cast gargoyles were positioned about. One looked like an aborted fetus. I noted a supply catalog titled "Medieval Gargoyles" tossed in a wastebasket, the obvious source of these mail-order monsters. A clock without a face, just a golden hour hand, and a pendulum swinging away the minutes and hours as if it were beheading them as they occurred hung on the wall. But the most beautiful part of the experience was the dreamy electronic music that played on an endless loop throughout the room and, it turned out, throughout the entire house. Its aery musings made me feel as if I were a lava lamp filled with rising and falling lumps of congealed ruby red gummy drops.

"Heere iss a sponge," said Carlos as he thrust toward me a gigantic orange sponge that looked as if it had just been yanked off a coral reef. "Now you will get to work."

But instead of pointing me in the direction of any specific task, my latest zombie master pushed me down onto the plush carpeting on all fours. He tied about my head a leather mask, then snapped blindfolds into place, then a pacifier down my throat that snapped on as well. I felt the familiar collar and leash applied about the neck. He forced me to crawl in many directions by tugging on my chain. It was like being in a fabulously complex labyrinth or being a member of a fierce high school marching band, to the right, to the right, to the left left right. I always suspected that the hacienda was not so large. But I never actually saw the place laid out. Instead I was led on my knees on this blind escapade through a maze of my master's invention.

Suddenly I was in the bathroom. An obvious enough location. Blinders unsnapped. I did a bit of desultory sponging of the white tile floor. I noted a cologne bottle with a hand-carved wooden skull for its stopper. A primitive control switch was marked with labels made from a label gun for "vent," "hot," etc., making the room a bit scary. Then I was blinded again. My next appearance was in the bedroom. Nancy was lying on a vast black water bed, changing the channels on a TV that was perched on a little ledge like a sur-veillance camera. I sponged down a few white cabinets. By now she was paying me scant attention. I suspected from her eyes that Carlos had given her some pills that were making her happy. What a lovely sight she made. She was spaced-out. I respected her.

I crawled into a walk-in closet where Carlos, or Raw, was playing with his computer. "Seat down and I let you watch," he said softly. By now he'd removed his paisley bathrobe and put on his camou-flage fatigues. He did have an amazing computer uni-verse at his beck and call. He'd made his own movie in which the name *Carlos* was spelled out in metal letters turned every which way in the void of illusionary space. He showed me a grid, like a prison, filled with images of boys. They looked much like me. They were boys with sweet faces. One was roped to a St. Andrew's cross. One's chain was being tugged as he stared at the camera, dumb as an oyster, silent as a clam. He was a desirable piece of merchandise with an unfortunate nine-yard stare.

"You're a zombie, you should be able to help me solve this puzzle because you can't think of anything else." Nancy let out a yelp of pleasure from the nearby water bed. I thought Carlos's comment particularly insensitive, as I of course had no powers of concentration or problem solving. I felt this was an excuse for his showing off. The "puzzle" he was referring to was a computer game. He led us into a graphic depiction of a pyramid's inner sanctum. By touching the stones around a circular well, one could summon up a mind game fixed in the center of the blue waters. He had aced many of them, his accomplishments awarded with diamonds that circled a mandala of stone and water. The mission he was having trouble with involved matching up six pairs of objects, which included a scythe, a bench, a bowl, a comb, a hammer, a wooden case. Were they to be matched by material? By use? By appearance? This was the question driving him nuts.

The game show announcer with the voice of a pharaoh had given two so-called clues.

"You do not need to know the names to these here things. If you ask me this, this I shall tell." He was referring to a trick whereby if you clicked onto the object, the name would be announced in full echo.

"These objects must be matched in six pairs in order to achieve the diamond tiara."

Well, I was of course the last person on earth, or one of them, to solve such a problem. I had almost no strategic capabilities. I lived outside of all detail, all machination, all problem solving. He was doing this to tease me, to prepare me for my entry into the sarcophagus of sarcophagi, the room of fellowship I'd been searching for so listlessly for so long.

The music continued to space us out as we walked and crawled to the final room. I was masked again. I was pushed to the floor in a disoriented condition. I think Carlos snapped a few of the gelatin capsules Nancy was enjoying so much into my own pale gray dog bowl of water, which he so graciously plopped in front of my face while we watched a made-for-computer movie about a grab bag of spicy topics: pyramids, ghosts, alien abductions. The journey into the next room was made sufferable by the blindness.

When I finally arrived in what felt like the darkest crawl space possible, he snapped off my eye patches. I was awed by the sights. The sweet and endlessly repetitive spacey music was continuing to haunt every arch and bone of my body. The lights were again ruby red. Three other boys were entranced there. The walls were covered in black carpeting. The lumber was unvarnished, basic pale wood. Two zombies were immediately visible. One was strapped onto a St. Andrew's cross, the X-shaped type on which he was being eternally twirled as if on a circular rotisserie. One was hanging on a pillory with his arms and ankles tied into a stretch so that he was the X rather than conforming to the X. Carlos then crawled me round to a pink-lit room behind prison bars where another boy was curled. The only other furniture in the cell was a hanging black Everlast boxing bag and a pumpkin shaved into the face of a happy demon.

"You guys will get to know each other later," he promised.

He showed me to my new domicile, with which I was infinitely well pleased, no regrets. It was like arriving home for the first time. It was an exact reproduction of a sarcophagus built for the mummy of a pharaoh. Carlos had designed its cover on his computer. It was painted gold. The eyes were closed. He bound me round and round in silver duct tape so that I was unable to move. My head was bandaged in silver as well except for holes crudely cut for eyes, nose, and mouth. "Moving is for humans," he said. Then he laid me out in this tomb. It was like being buried in the shape of a paramecium. What was most beautiful about it—the cover art—quickly became invisible to my eyes. The top was shut down on me. I realized instantly that there was a little fan above my head blowing fresh air into my freshly dug grave. I could feel that there was some sort of exhaust fan below my feet as well that was drawing the revivifying airs over my immobile body. Most inventive was a concave video monitor a few inches above my face. Sometimes it flashed on the other boys. Sometimes it went gray, blank, pointillist. I knew then that Carlos was watching my eyes, perhaps from his water bed. The tomb of the living! The music was piped through speakers situated next to my receptive ears. I swooned to the exaggerated angelic tunes.

The music softened to a simple electronic harp. The screens flashed more slowly and clearly on each of my paralyzed roommates. I began to hear their personal sounds piped into my shallow grave. I heard stomach rumblings, throat clearings, heavy breathing. I could practically hear their itches. I suspected that these very discomforts made them as happy inside as I was. Something was happening! We were talking! We were talking to each other! It was like a chorus of disembodied lost souls. How beautiful it was! I was feeling I belonged. A crying sensation traveled all through my arms and legs.

"I'm David, I'm a flight attendant," one of them was saying. He was the one curled in the pink light of the cell. That one video screen in my coffin was in color, the rest were black and white.

"How did you find out you were a zombie?" the one slumped in chains was asking.

"Whenever I went on camping trips with my friends, I was designated to carry all the tents and bags and equipment on my back like a workhorse, and I never questioned it or thought why."

"You were a beast of burden?"

"My name is Harry," said the one slumped in chains. "A couple years ago when I was about twenty I noticed that no hair had ever grown on my body and that my penis was that of a boy of four, even though I was shapely."

"That's more like some physical manifestation of being a zombie," the one swirling slowly on the X cross was saying. "My name is Handkerchief. I used to try to sleep every night when I was eight with my best friend. My favorite would be to get down on the floor near his feet. Or in the middle of the night bury my head in his behind. He never said boo about it. It was like he was putting up with some strangeness in me."

"I'm Zero!" I cried out exultantly. As soon as I yelled it, I just started bawling practically. "I'm Zero!" I repeated. "I'm so glad not to be alone with my aloneness anymore. We are an ancient race, of that I'm sure." Then I started bawling again. I had discovered my true zombie name: Zero.

"What are your symptoms?" Handkerchief asked conciliatorily from the cross.

We all started talking to each other at once. The chorus began. It wasn't like a conversation of different personalities. Because we were zombies we didn't have those sorts of projected differences. We hadn't staked out much personal space for ourselves. We lived erased. But the release was palpable. It was a backward, primitive, dark nirvana where everything was one. It was like being in the ocean before the sexes had differentiated themselves and everyone was either feeding or being fed on, fucking or being fucked over. But there were no nervous systems yet to tell apart the differences. There were no early-warning systems. Only the stimulation of constant danger and constant hope.

"It's like there's nothing to talk about."

"Yeah. It's great to talk to someone who doesn't feel like there's anything so great about talking."

"What we do is more like barking than talking."

"I would never hurt anybody."

"I never said a nasty thing to anybody."

"I never fucked a boy or a girl. Nor ever was fucked in return. But I've seen lots of it. Because of the kind of people I hang out with, I guess."

"I've never seen a movie in a movie theater. Only on video."

"I never played a board game. Only computer games."

"What do you think of Carlos?"

"He's strong and beautiful like the wind in the trees."

"Or the lightning that breaks the head of the roof of the house."

"I love the way those sutures on his chest must be from a knife wound or a bullet hole."

"Like the bullet holes in the president's palace."

"Nancy and Carlos are definitely *Not* zombies."

"Has anyone ever had a master before?"

I heard a loud gasp.

"Ha! Yes!"

"Yes!"

"Yes! Yes!"

"But seriously . . ."

"Yes. Let's get to the serious part while we have this rare chance."

"What is at the bottom of this? Is it Jesus? Buddha?"

"You didn't know?"

"It's the *Ancient Zombie Religion*."

"It's from Africa. The gods are called *loas*."

"They help with life's daily problems. In return they must be served with ceremonies, offerings of food and drink, and occasionally animal sacrifice."

"But because we're suburban boys from America, we have new zombie possibilities. Our *loas* are often other humans, but humans of another strain who are meant to be divine governors. Their emblem is the gold watch of the hypnotist."

"That's their nice emblem. Their bad emblem is the ax of the executioner."

"What did we do to deserve our place?"

"There is no deserving, only serving the blind pattern."

"The essence of voodoo is keeping in harmony with the *loas*, the dead, and nature."

"The main thing is dancing to the drums."

"You should be here on the Day of the Dead in November. You can see the *loas*. They can be seen in cemeteries or roaming the streets, dressed like corpses or undertakers to guard us from being blinded by their pure visibility, by visible darkness."

"The lords of death and the cemetery, they mock human vanity and pretension, and remind people that sex is the source of life."

"Been there, done that," I joked. How unlike me to tell a joke. This therapy was working its magic on me.

"But seriously. We're a new permutation."

"Duh." Handkerchief was telling a joke there, too. We were obviously all lightening up.

"It's the return back to the beginning of the cycle, so that it is the spirituality of the next age. But you will never find it here in Haiti, among the nineteenth-century versions. They were political. And led to the slave revolts."

I suddenly realized that Sir Edward the M.D. was a *loa*. And Control Freak. And even the boy Mark from long ago.

"We are here to return to slavery, to extend our arms for the handcuffs and shackles to be put in place. All because of the inner feeling of rightness this gives us."

"It was a holiness that began to be felt in the American suburbs and has only spread. Its minor chord of weirdness always takes a while to catch on. But catch on it will."

"I have worshiped the shark," I said.

"Of course you have."

"But the greatest shark of all is invisible. It's the predator that eats us and everyone. And in being eaten we are most fully sated."

"Wow!"

That's when the drumming began. The electronic harp was replaced by recurring drums. First one by itself. Then a series. Then clumps. Until pretty soon the stuff was thick and congested as a heart after a hit of one of Sir Edward the M.D.'s poppers. I was having an amyl nitrate rush from the music. It became a fusion of the most primitive drumming and droning, the kind I did naturally every night as I fell asleep, the kind my father used to punish me for by turning on all the electric lights in my bedroom until I stopped droning for good. It was a fusion of drumming and droning with rock guitar and keyboard. There began to be lyrics screaming for political change, some in English, the rest in a language of gobbledygook. Their words were birds flying solo: *Ram, Boukan Ginen, Foula, Sanba-Yo, Koudjay.*

Crash! Suddenly I heard speakers crashing. The music was swallowed up in a gulp by a silence full of the static of rushing and banging. The air was stopped up in my sarcophagus. The images on the video screen froze, then died in a purple haze. I was frightened that there had been an electricity failure and that now I was finally to die of suffocation.

Death. What a terrible thought to have, and for many of us it is as if it is our only thought. All the rest are just window dressing.

Luckily just then the lid snapped open. I saw to my horror that the chains were being undone. Carlos was hurriedly unlocking the padlock to the gate of the pink prison cell. My friends were being dragged away like lumpy laundry bags. Finally Carlos knocked over my coffin so that I tumbled onto the floor, no breakage. Nancy hurried over in a shriek to undo me, naked, from all the wrappings of gauze and tape. As she was doing so, and dressing me hastily, she whispered in my ear, "The old-fashioned zombie masters are mad at Carlos. They're sending their minions to do away with him. They don't like the new style. How stupid! You unfortunately are their targets! It's like killing the cattle to rattle the rancher. Or leaving a horse's head in someone's bed."

As we rushed out the front of the house, I observed that the weather had changed dramatically. It was as if the heavens were smoking a gigantic cigar and blowing all the smoke in our faces. I could barely make out the activities on the ground. I saw that Handkerchief was being loaded into the back of Nancy's Jeep. I'm not sure where the other two went. Coming up the dirt road were hundreds of these shufflers in pajamas. I looked into their faces for a quiet moment when time was put on pause, I forget why. And I did see true peace, the kind that I'd felt for hours and days in the twilight of Control Freak's apartment. I did bond with them, or their mood. They were the most curious kinds of enemies to have. It was as if all these beautiful angels with big white wings appeared and just pulled out machine guns from under their white gowns and started gunning down innocent people.

Carlos shoved me into the trunk of his car, which was a light blue Haitian police car. I curled there while the lid was smashed down, and the rumbling and shaking began that let me know we were navigating the ups and downs of a smashed rocky road I'd seen before with my eyes. I felt as if we were in a chase scene, but I saw nothing of the chasing. All was an endless backlit gray. The dusty oxygen decreased, decreased, decreased, until it was a mere whiff I could barely smell. I missed the tiny fans at my head and feet in the sarcophagus. Finally arrived the moment I'd been anticipating, all the ride, if not all my life. A bang shot my head back into the hard metal edge of a device used to crank up spent tires to change them. I had no spare room. So I went out. I didn't see stars. Something more like asteroids in video games. A rumble of them. And then I was dead to the car.

I don't remember how I got to the plane. I have a visceral memory of Carlos holding me sloppily in his arms as he ran and I flapped. I certainly don't know anything about the ticketing. I mean, I had a one-way ticket. Remember? I do remember Nancy saying, "Oh, if only I could sing him lullabies until he woke up again. I hate seeing him hurt!" She was a true human woman. I love her in that audio memory.

I never saw any of my fellow zombies again. I don't know how they fared. I watched a nondescript boy of a man who looked ageless in a brown topcoat and sneakers gunned down on the tarmac. That might have been Handkerchief. I saw blood clot on his topcoat. When the plane took off and was a mile high I saw a flash on the ground. Our pilot, with an accent similar to Carlos's, said over the intercom that a passenger plane had been blown up prior to takeoff. Probably by a terrorist suicide bomber, he speculated. And then I was out again. Drifting and swaying, my body approaching a buzz saw at the end of an assembly line to which I was strapped, then drawing back or being drawn back somehow again. How strange to be protected and abused in the same stroke.

Eventually I came to. We had entered a holding pattern above John F. Kennedy Airport in New York City. No one was sitting next to me.

What's that?

I looked down and saw a note, like a luggage identification tag, tied on a string around my neck. It read: "Don't forget what you saw and heard! Feel nothing. Experience everything."

This note became my one and only possession.

Chapter 14

Conclusion: How Zombie got to the bottom of time.

THE WALK BACK to the city was not so eventful. It would have been easier if it had been August instead of October. I appreciated the care my father had taken when he put me on the bus. He must have known that it arrived at the Port Authority in mid-town and was quite convenient to all locations. Just making it by foot from the John F. Kennedy Airport the day I bungled off the plane from Haiti to the spot where I had *begun* my search on my first arrival a few years earlier took a good seven hours. They ignored me again in Customs, the man with tan-tinted military eyeglasses barely glancing at me as I walked past him, luckily since I had no passport. When I set out from the terminal, trying to dodge my way slowly across a daisy chain of intersecting arrival and departure ramps for taxis and cars, the sun was white as the moon, white hot, and high in the sky, beating down on my bare shoulders (except for the straps of my pale blue T-shirt).

"Do you know the way to downtown New

York City?" I had asked a brusque skycap at the airport. He glowered back at me as if I were a ghost. I didn't know I could scare a chicken, let alone a man in an imposing uniform with a stylish cap. Then I recognized him as Haitian. Maybe he *was* seeing a ghost, as far as Haitian culture taught.

"Just follow the green signs on the side of the road," he told me.

That's what I did. I walked past rows and rows of white tombstones lined up like soldiers. I passed tall smokestacks exhaling gray puffs aggressively into the air. I traversed nice sections of matching brick double blocks on streets lined by scuffed trees. I stopped at one intersection where there were so many kinds of sirens—ambulance, police car, a car being broken into. This is like a more technologically advanced Haiti! I remember thinking. Things were a bit mellower when I made it over a heavily trafficked bridge into the central quarter of Manhattan. When I arrived the sun was an orange bloodshot circle in a purple sky.

By the time the sunlight had been turned off, I was finally wobbling through the uneven streets again of the villages of Manhattan, east and west. It was actually cold following the autumn sunset. My sandals were worn to two thin pieces of colorless paper. My cutoffs were fried. They hung on me like the battered skin of a Kentucky Fried Chicken—I'd had one as my last meal in a box at the airport. A

BRAD GOOCH

beggar handed it to me as a hand-me-down he didn't want. His eyes were more ablaze with the possibilities of cold cash to buy heroin with. He told me that since I'd left—I told him a little of my story, not the whole shazaam—the heroin on the streets had become so powerful that you didn't need a needle to shoot, you could just snort it like coke.

"That's a great expense saver," the beggar informed me gleefully. I thought to myself that Sir Edward the M.D. must be sharing in his mirth right now.

Reminded so much of my first exciting trip to New York City a few years back when I was still green salad, not yet chopped meat, I of course thought to head over to the Little Prison of the Château de Sade, where such kindnesses had initially been showered on me when I was in much the same sinking boat of a life circumstance. Remember Wendy the feminist bartender who introduced me to Sir Edward the M.D.? Of course you remember *him*. Who could forget that human lamppost, that cardboard skeleton hanging on someone's door on Halloween? But when I arrived at the steps that led down to the Little Prison of the Château de Sade there was alas a chain slung across with a blank metal sign hanging across on which was scrawled in tiny letters the message "This place of business has been discontinued by order of the City Government of New York, which regulates all of Manhattan. In its place please turn right around, walk down the street in the direction away from the polluted river, until you arrive at a cobblestone street about three blocks away and a set of steps going down until you hit a sign for the club Crypt. You'll be happy there."

I was indeed happy for the sign. I remember when I was a young zombie playing board games in which I played both sides—I had the unusual ability to forget what I knew from being the opponent when playing his opposite. I could play both sides of a chessboard, too. My weird and useless skill had something to do with zero investment in winning or losing. Anyway, I followed the scrawled directions, and they turned out to have been correct. There on the side of the wall was a spooky sign of red letters spelling out "Crypt" in bloody script. A young black man sat on a stool at the top of the stairs.

"What's up?" he asked.

"I followed the sign here."

"Go downstairs and try your luck," he grumbled.

I understood his hesitation when I arrived at the foot of the stairs and turned into the ticket sales office. Sitting behind a double thickness of glass panes was the greeter and door guard. He was a bit weighty, with gray hair.

"That'll be thirty dollars," he coughed from a place in his belly.

"I don't have any money, sir," I said in a slumped manner.

"What *do* you have?" he asked.

I don't usually say or do the right thing, but at that particular moment I had a storm in my placid brain. And when I said it I said it loud. And this was it: "I wonder if Wendy the feminist works here."

Well I couldn't have said anything faster or better if it had been beat in my head by a true zombie master.

"Well, yes, as a matter of fact she does," he said, surprised. He waddled off in his green jeans to look into the matter.

When he returned, Wendy the feminist was accompanying him. She looked so sharp. Her brunette hair was cropped short. Her man's white shirt was tied above the belly button (an outie). Her Daisy Mae blue jeans were like skin. And the boots went without saying in such an establishment as this.

"Remember me?" I croaked, putting all my hopes and fears into that one question. It was a rare moment of identity for me. I was so used to not being remembered. And she answered back as graciously and as full of judgment and of as much understanding as could be expected to be mustered at such an uncomplicated moment with no past and no future, at least as far as she was concerned. For me, both past and future hung in the balance.

"No," she said.

"I'm Zombie, you hooked me up once with Sir Edward the M.D.," I pleaded.

"Zooooombie," she squealed in a completely

dreamy reversal of her previous position. "Zombie," she reiterated to the dark winds being churned by a standing fan.

And then it all began. The love affair of the night, the week, the year. The proof that it was a love affair, such as I had never known, was that it led to a job. Wendy the feminist took me in. She took me in that night to the club, for free. She took me into her confidence. And mostly she took me so far in that eventually I was allowed to stay there, to work there, to become the very caretaker of the crypt. I had never had a job before, and certainly not one with such a weight of responsibility. Wendy set it all up for me. But that happened later, or soon enough, at what was called "the end of the night," though in the final phase into which I moved the notion of ends or beginnings, of hours or phases, took on less and less meaning, zero meaning, I suppose would describe it best.

After I got the hang of it, I almost enjoyed my newly invented job—better during the afternoons when no one was there. I'd wake up about noon in the big cage they had set up for fantasy scenes. I didn't know what the particular fantasy was. For me it was just a home, and an unusually comfortable one. Much more comfortable than the garage I lived in as a youth, where the wind would whistle through the broken windows and the smell of car oil on the stone floor would make me puke some nights. I was living in an olfactory nightmare and barely even knew it.

Here all was warm and encoded with messages of peace and tranquillity.

So, as I was saying, I would wake up around noon. I guess it was noon. There was certainly no light in that basement. I would wash up and pee in the men's room, so busy at nights with customers doing drugs and splashing excess beer around as if they were firemen with hoses. The same, I suppose, happened in the ladies' room, though I know they don't have hoses. I wasn't allowed in there. Even though I had no particular allegiance to any sex or proclivity, I was still identified as one of the men. At least in regards to which cabin I could use to relieve myself.

One particular morning I awoke to find that Wendy had thoughtfully taped two photocopied pages from two different books to the poles of my cell. She was very learned. She was actually studying "the History of Women" at NYU, where she was well on her way to earning a doctorate in Woman. She told me there were no doctorates in zombie, and indeed not even a single course or a single mention in any course in the school's catalog. That certainly put me in my place, not to any great surprise. I'd been in that place now for what seemed like aeons. One of them was from a book about dreams. She had high-lighted in yellow the entry under *Z* for zombie: "Zombies represent those who allow others to con-trol them through psychological ploys and the manipulation of fear. They are a warning to the dreamer to stop believing everything he or she is told." I understood the first sentence; not the second.

I moved on to the next tattered piece of second-hand paper with the next entry. This was from some other book by the same author, a book made of questions followed by her answers. (Wendy read books written only by women authors. I know of no books written by zombies. This is the first!) The question she asked herself and answered for us all was "Can the dead come back to life like a zombie?" They should be so unlucky, was my improvised answer to myself. I was actually chuckling with glee at that. How rare an event, I realized. What a better mood I was in since I had met my blank brothers in Haiti.

Here was the author's own, more serious, gloomy, even, answer: "The questioner's concept is a contradiction. Zombies don't 'come back to life' because they were never really dead in the first place. Zombies are evidence of the result of a powerful botanical's effect upon the human system, which produces the state of a deathlike stupor. Now in this deathlike stupor, the perpetrator (or sorcerer, as he is called) digs up the buried body and forces another powerful drug into the system. The buried body flutters his eyes and is helped out of the grave. He walks. He is then perceived as 'the undead.' But the sorcerer who has the drugs can now control the zombie because of the mental stupor his drug induces in the

victim. See? There is really no 'dead' person involved
. . . only those who have been made to appear dead.
An adept sorcerer who utilizes these powerful botan-
icals to effect a waking-state hypnosis in another can
literally erase the individual's emotions, memories,
values, and attitudes, thereby obtaining total control
over the victim. Know that no physically dead person
can ever be brought back to life, as said feat is
accomplished through the will and the hand of God
alone."

Poppycock, I thought to myself, having no idea
what that word meant. I later asked Wendy what it
meant and she looked it up in the dictionary
overnight and returned the next day to tell me it
meant "soft dung," from "pap" for soft, and "*kak*"
for dung, in some dead ancient language. I had
always just thought it was a goofy flower with a
clown's hat on. Anyway, the point is that she was
talking about things she'd read in books. But at best
they were books dealing with those dusty old zombies I'd seen lumbering down the road in Haiti like a
troupe of unemployed character actors whom col-
orization had left in a lurch: they were definitely only
black-and-white material. In their place was something much more mysterious, more devious, more
unexplained, more of the moment, more disturbing,
funnier: me. And, if they exist, my kind. Enough of
that, I thought, and tossed the papers in a can.

Large dust balls sailed through the many rooms

of the Crypt. I slowly turned on electric wall switch after electric light and set to work. I carefully cleaned out my own cell first. Then I turned my attention to the bar with its piles of Styrofoam and plastic cups, in which were served only beer and light fruity beverages. (The bartendress's name—at that bar—was really Bev, ha ha, for "beverage," I thought, ha ha.) Next I carefully cleaned this fake Harley motorcycle they had where whippers and spankers liked to drape their willing supplicants to make their behinds feel worse than ever. I totally blew the haze of dust away, and then I shined and shined. It was clean! It was ready for violations and violence. The wooden Puritan's scaffold was fine the way it was. Maybe some cherry polish. But not today. I then moved on to the back room with the bar that would be presided over that night by Wendy. I made it gleam. (Didn't I, Wendy? If she's reading this, she's an old lady by now. Diiiidn't I, Weeeendy?) All that was left were the lines of pink cubicles on both sides of a hallway to nowhere. I soaped them out. I polished the chains that could be slung across to make them occupied. These were voluntary cubes of mutually satisfactory prostitution in which both partners were unpaid prostitutes, a democracy in action. But I'm getting fuller and fuller of these chirps and chitters ever since I came back from Haiti, aren't I?

The day was worn to a nub with my dusting and scrubbing and polishing. I was getting the heart, liver and lungs of the place ready for the larger body that was the Evening and then the unruly Giant of the Night, whose organs were self-sustaining and self-feeding and self-eviscerating finally, but that is much, much later. Finally Wendy arrived with dinner and conversation.

"Puppy," she said.

"Oh, Wendy," I yelped as I dived for her ankles to hug and kiss them. It had been so long since I'd seen her. And she was my contact now. I never went aboveground anymore. She was toting my dinner. I hadn't eaten since the last time I'd seen her. There's not much food underground. Nutrition, perhaps, but not food. She'd brought a glistening plastic box in which there were all sorts of foods I needed and craved. "Korean," she informed me, indicating that the box was carried from a certain shop I'd never seen with my own eyes but knew existed through the textural map of the food she brought me from there. Come to think of it, I don't think she ever brought me food from anywhere else. It was ritualistic. And that's why it was good food for me.

The menu: broccoli, California roll, pink snips of ginger, rolls of duck, potatoes baked in ultraviolet light, orange rings, pineapple rings, mashed potatoes, onion rings, pounds of maca-roni, scads of chili con carne—how did that get in there?—applesauce extraordinaire, snap peas, corn devoid of its buttress—and this is how we lived!—spinach stretched to its limit, gargantuan impossible shrimp, flounder lit from the inside, blood juice from beef that had been shed by an unimaginable butcher in who knew where, love, I mean olives, blue, black, and green, and there is nothing more to say, only to eat. Thanks, Wendy!

We talked, sitting in the shadows. Wendy was chewing gum. She was folding and unfolding a dollar bill in tight designs.

"How was your day, sweet Zombie?" she asked, kissing me on the forehead.

"It was beautiful," I answered, neutered somehow of all pain for a change.

"Most people wouldn't know how you can stand to live in the deep dark, but I understand," she said. "I understand because I'm a freak."

"You're not a freak, Wendy," I jumped in, as if to her defense.

"Oh, Zombie, you're just saying that," she said as she stroked my hairless arm.

"No, I'm not just saying that, I'm saying something else," I said nearly incomprehensibly.

"Can you tell me what you mean?"

"I mean that you're living, really living. Not like me, who doesn't have a life. And there's nothing freaky about that. It's the way everyone does it. Or . . . almost everyone."

"Oh, Zombie. You break my heart sometimes. I just want to take you by the hand and lead you out of all this. And I would do it for you if I could do it for myself."

"But I love it here, Wendy. With you, and all the circus performers whose club this is and who do it for free, for the sheer love of it."

"I sense that you are happy, Zombie. For the first time in your life, perhaps. Much happier than when you showed up that first night at the Little Prison of the Château de Sade. So maybe it's better to be more fully dead. Maybe by being more fully dead, you're actually more fully alive. Maybe you're just dead to something, but not to everything. Obviously, since you're breathing. And maybe by not feeling anything, you feel more. Maybe you're tingling. Maybe you're right."

"I don't know, Wendy. It's not like I haven't thought about these things more than you could possibly know. But I haven't come up with answers. Because I'm it. I'm in it. So how can I say? When people are in hurricanes, are they what they think they thought they were? What the people thought the hurricanes were, I mean? I'm sure not."

"Oh, Zombie, you're so learned. You're like an old soul."

"I don't have a soul, Wendy."

"But how can someone so soulful not have a soul?"

"But it goes back to what somebody said. Was it me who said it or you?"

"Oh, you adorable little Boy Scout, you!"

And then she did it again. She leaned over and gave me a big squeeze that sent stabs of joy and cries of biological glee shooting through my body. Wendy simply pushed all my buttons. I think she made that remark about Boy Scouts because I was dressed in my standard evening uniform: brown shorts, dark green T-shirt, black sandals with white socks. I had made it up myself based on a summer uniform a UPS driver had worn down to the basement one morning. He woke me up. It was so rare to have a visitor at that hour. He was delivering some sort of summons for the owner. I was apparently— Wendy later told me—the perfect caretaker because I hadn't a clue who the owner was, didn't even know there was one, had never given a thought to his existence. There was apparently something shady about him that he preferred to keep hidden. But of course how would we have gotten here if there wasn't an owner? Stupid of me. I loved his UPS uniform. He didn't love me because he had to leave without my signing. But I took a lot away from him. For him I was a curlicue in his day. For me he was an explosion, like a man falling to earth and forming a crater at my very feet or something.

Before it's time to go to work there were a few matters I wanted to linger on, really as a way of lingering on that feeling of Wendy rubbing my back, and kissing my neck, and making love to my ears by nibbling on them. Now I can't remember the thoughts. Maybe there weren't any. I confided all this one night to a member of the club Crypt. He told me that he had the same experience on laughing gas at the dentist's office. That he was filled to the brim with insights he wanted to carry back to tell to his mistress and to his boss. When he walked down the street away from the dentist's office, he felt as if he were looking into a crumpled brown paper bag with none of the expected bits of candy in it. Impressive, huh? He laughed and laughed. I didn't actually get the point of that story. Maybe I missed a few salient points. It was time to work.

"Kiss me, honey, they're here." That was Wendy speaking.

She was speaking about the other employees beginning to roll in, but I stopped her from putting herself and everyone in motion.

"I remember what I wanted to ask," I spurted out. "What about Sir Edward the M.D.? Whatever happened to him? Will he ever scold us and make our lives hell again? Ha! Ha!"

"Oh, Zombie, yes. Let me think." She grew quiet. "He was my boyfriend for a while. But I found him incredibly reserved and distant, like a dictionary. He never laid a hand on me. . . ."

"Never laid a hand on you??" I shrieked. It was a lesson in how different people were different with different other ones. I never knew that.

"But I respect him, and he shows up here sometimes, sweetie, and I'm sure he will come to play again a part in a triangle with us. Which probably means that he was involved with us in a triangle in another life."

"But it can't mean that," I interjected, not having had another life. "I can't have had another life if I don't have a soul."

"But what's all this religious searching if you don't have a soul? You're so spiritual!" she practically shrieked, cheapening a bit what was and is an important moment between us.

"I found my soul in the soullessness of the primitive spirituality of possession and rote performance in which slavery is liberation," I said, managing a mouthful of words that seemed to have a life of their own as they spewed out of my open mouth. "It makes the seconds count."

"Oh," Wendy said, getting bored already. It was reaaally time to go to work now. We actually wanted to go to work. Who wants to sit around and talk or think? Ugh! Yeeech! Vomit! Or worse yet, do it at a dinner table in restaurants with windows so big that anyone driving by could shoot at you, or in basements so deep that if a fire was ever lit from one of those little big fat jerks' fat cigars, the whole place would incinerate with you in it. Not that I'd ever been there or done that. But Wendy told me some things, some experiences of hers, that clued me in quite well. Quite, quite well.

That night at the Crypt was particularly warm, friendly, and intimate. It was couples night for a bit at the beginning, which seemed to put everyone in a closer mood. Then all the types moved in, looking for breath and flesh and blood and ideas and all the things these kinds of people are on the prowl for. They practically seethe with invisible pictures that are framed inside their craniums that no one else can see but which, if visible, would predict and explain their mysterious behaviors. I certainly couldn't see them. But then I'd always felt that way when my parents took me to drive-ins; the second feature was usually a cheap European dubbed love story, and I never understood exactly what the unseen forces were that were driving the main characters to slit their throats or fall asleep or run screaming through the rain after a bus. It was truly as if they were possessed by *loas*—I know that now, of course, only with my further Haitian education. When someone guessed what invisible picture was in their mind, then all love and hell broke loose. It was like a masked ball for mind readers. A holiday for autistic people. A loose-limbed dance macabre.

A lot of the women looked like schoolteachers, like she who had originally taught Mark *David Copperfield*. Will I ever forget her forbidding shoes? But most of these were thinner. She was sturdier. Not that there weren't sturdy women here. But the ones I'm thinking of were tall, with prominent cheekbones and ashen hair tied back. They always seemed to be having their feet kissed and caressed by men on their knees who looked as if they had been slow students in the real-life classrooms of their pasts before they figured out how to make some dough by operating dutifully within the system. (I certainly never even got that far.)

Once when I was polishing the brass rail under a bar where the customers rested their feet—a favorite job of mine, as it was nearby beloved Wendy, I sensed her heat through the bar—I heard the loud peal of a hysterical scream. I banged my head as I lurched up. Even with my extremely low blood pressure I was triggered into an immediate reaction by the shrill alarm. Everyone else practically stampeded into one flat wall or corner or friend or stranger or another. There at an intersection between a hallway and the room of the second bar where I was working away, a woman in a black cat suit was hissing at a man in the stupidest striped shirt, dirty linen pants, and wisps of remaining hair.

They were being kept apart by a gentleman who seemed as if he were from one of the islands near Haiti—Cuba or Puerto Rico. Carlos, with more meat on his bones. His black T-shirt announced that he was a *MONITOR*, though the letters were stuck on inaccurately so that some were not on line with others. I was mindful of Halloween in the grade school playground and those whose mothers had done a good pressing job and those whose hadn't. His hadn't. Or had I pressed on those letters? She started whaling on the insufficient man in the striped shirt of the Arrow brand.

"How dare you touch me? How dare you speak to me? Who are you? Who gave you permission? You are a worm. You are a wormhole. You have no right to invade the private and sacred space of my body and the area immediately surrounding it like flies!"

Whoa! The Catwoman had certainly not met her match.

"I'm sorry," he murmured, and resumed his caterpillar walk.

(I remembered briefly a scene I'd seen one eventless afternoon at Control Freak's recording studio of a home. It was called "a Zen moment." Maybe this was a comedy show and not the news broadcast I remembered it to be. Several Japanese waiters were holding little yellow chickadees on the wooden balcony of the restaurant where they served. They would release the little birdies into the waters of the lagoon surrounding the serene establishment. Then crocodiles appeared from below and started snapping the birdies into their mouths and swallowing them down. Snap and swallow. Snap and swallow. It was beautiful, like colored balloons being popped by children in their mouths at a birthday party. Crocodiles are hatched, too, just like chickadees, just like babies from the tummies of mummies. And then it was over. The music was new age. The kind that puts you to sleep if you're not being eaten yourself. Something to bliss out on. The music, I mean. Not the fate of the poor little chickadees.)

I relaxed back down and began shining the bronze. Soon it was brilliant enough that I could see something like a face in it. I imagined it must be mine. But I had never been one to look at myself in the mirror. Was there really anything to see?

"What was her name?" I jolted up, definitely hitting my head this time again, then repeating the question.

"Whose name?" Wendy smiled sweetly as she poured a nonalcoholic beer into a plastic urine sample cup. "Whose name, sweetie?"

"The girl in Peter Pan?" I asked.

"Why, Wendy," she answered.

"And that's your name. That's what I thought."

"It took you long enough."

"I'm not exactly fast. But I get there, and get there I do."

"Like the tortoise and the hare."

"Huh?"

"Don't worry, that's another story. You can ask me about it in five years."

"Hah!"

It was my job, too, to wander around. Partly this was to keep me from falling asleep. I would finally discover when the last person had left if I kept walking around and then be able to close the grillwork of the front door and resume my daily nocturnal existence. Wendy asked me to walk around in case the owner was on the premises. The owner liked all his employees to be smack happy and ready for wear. "Smack happy and ready for wear" was a direct quotation from the owner, Wendy said. So I did. Along the way I saw many marvelous sights. Not since the shark feed had I been so amazed by the sheer explosion of the circus we live in.

An elephant of a woman was there getting her elephant behind smacked. She was short and entirely overweight and not over thirty-five. But she liked to shimmy out of her skirt and show this behind, which did entirely resemble the behind of an elephant trained to perch on a stool where a trainer would lash the thing with a whip of a stick. A trainer who of course sported a villain's mustache. As did so many of the men who lurked on the premises of the club Crypt night after night. They were pirates. Their treasure was flesh. Their ships were off course. They never cashed in because they had been too appropriated by the values of the ships they were attacking to be truly set free. They were bad boys. And they were whipping the sometimes elephantine bad girls. But not always elephantine. Sometimes the women ruled by the beauty of the incomprehensibility of their motives. Whoever's motives were the most incomprehensible were the most beautiful. I loved these people. I'm not being at all arch in what I say. I loved them more than I had ever loved any *group* of human beings.

Whenever there was a white man and an

African American woman, the white man was kneeling before the African American woman. I never saw
an exception to this rule, though I looked and looked.
One of my favorites was the African American
woman who wore a halter top of leopard skin with
her belly showing and below the tight blue pants that
women wear when they're on the street way late and
below those the high heels that women wear at the
same time, same place.

"Loooovely," the young white man said who
was kneeling in front of the very dark crèche of her
body. I would judge from his accent that he hailed
from Long Island, this thin caricature of a human in
white chinos and other white apparel, but then
everyone to me is a kind of a caricature because I've
never understood what made the supposedly deep
and transparently divine human run. But he went on:

"I mean, I prefer black-black the way you are,"
said the kneeler. "The way the pencil stub is when
you dig it into the white paper to sign your name.
Not that chocolatey chocolate they all rave about.
And certainly not that nigger white-black of women
who are denying that which is subtlest in their soul.
I would never kneel at the pussy of a black woman
who was denying her heritage baked in the sun of the
jungle and coming out howling."

"Your talk curls my toes," his paramour answered,
sending him of course diving to separate her feet from
the bright red pumps resting atop a circular metal

support. (Meanwhile I wondered at the gentleman who could discern so many shades of black and brown and white and gray. I wondered if his true calling wasn't as an illustrator's colorist rather than as a lover.)

"If you walk past me again, I'm gonna plaster you through that wall."

The gentleman who spoke to me this way as I scurried past was quite handsome in a waxy slicked-back-black-hair way. He was dressed in all the paraphernalia of a motorcycle driver. He probably owned one of those bikes where the gas tank was painted the ludicrous color of flying Caribbean flamingos. (Caribbean flamingos are light orange rather than pink.) But I did believe him in all his cranky craziness. I did. And I never walked by there again. Why did he naturally hate me? Do you hate the usher who shows you, all popcorned, to your seats in the movie theater with a flashlight? But then either he was psychotically unbalanced, or the time of night and the locale allowed him to flash his psychotically unbalanced side. I never did anything to deserve this. Besides enter the exhibit at you know which museum.

A glamorous, arty, sophisticated, throaty woman was standing nearby that night, talking to a much less angular man. She was asking him what he did, more as a trap than as an invitation, it soon turned out. "I work in Internet, getting people into new areas for ads," he explained to her, leaving me baffled, but she caught on to the rough edges and let rip.

"I'm a distant type myself," she answered, again baffling me. "Not looking to get into anything tonight."

"I didn't say I wanted to marry you," he tried to joke.

"Oh, I'm already married," she jumped back at him.

"Where's your husband?" A natural question.

"I don't know."

An off-limits area behind a black rubber rope was reserved for the couples left over from the more matrimonial segment of the evening earlier. One man had somehow corraled two women to twirl together from a fishhook. Their breasts were fitted together like pieces of a puzzle. They were dressed in leather wraparounds, like gigantic black rubber bands. Their tormentor was peering at them through thick glasses, his tresses as complicated and as flowing as an old hippie's. He was joined by a helper who was equally creepy. They could have been radio talk-show hosts. Both in black leather vests made, it seemed, of a weave of leather and plastic. They both were whipping this marmalade of women's flesh. The leader had the twin feminine fish count monotonously every time a stripe was slashed into their backs. It was as if they were supposed to witness to the world of the club Crypt that they were in denial about what was going on, about the pain they were in. Other women walked up to guffaw at them while they praised them with the title "mistress" under duress. "Why's she calling me 'mistress'? Did you hear her call me 'mistress'?" one of their especially tormenting women friends started shouting to the ceiling. The lashes of her voice were perhaps more damaging to them than any of the nine tails of the cat whip being wielded by the unsightly radio announcer.

For a while his identical helper really did seem to be sticking teeny thumbtacks into their breasts. It couldn't have been. Or must have been a synthetic version of same, I thought hopefully. Then he smacked the tips of the tacks with a brush of a whip he swirled around mercilessly and full of good humor. The one with the most tacks was talking between her teeth. It was all testing. At the end he had her kneel in front of him and kiss his long black Florsheim shoes. She was thanking him between her teeth, too. All her rhetoric seemed to be a kind of feminine version of toughing it out, equally born of the insecurity of ordinary people.

Light fell like drops of rain on this scene of human need and heartrending responses followed by deprivations followed by something like love.

A boy in a collar. I mean a gay guy in a rhinestone collar.

An unshaved brute who had been in the navy was in my face. He wanted me to clean his car, called a "Pontiac Chevrolet." He wanted me to use something with a name like "vacuupump" on the interior of the wreck, which supposedly was filled, according

to him, with the debris of many nights at the movies
and of many women laid waste in the backseat. I did
want to do it and promised that the next time I sur-
faced I would. He was an unshaven soul with lots of
problems. He was alluring to a black woman at the
club. She made a fuss over his bicep's tattoo: a black
panther about to pounce on a tweetie bird. He told me
that on the street where he lives he's the only white
male. "It would look weird to have you visit me," he
said into my face with his stimulating garlic breath. It
was by way of explaining why I'd have to vacuum his
car parked on an esplanade on the West Side Highway
and clean the ketchup stains from off its rug.

"My shoes are broken scallops," someone really
and truly said to me. I don't know what he was on.
"Angel dust," he said. What a lovely name. And certainly the words were poetic enough to have been an
angel's.

A blond man in one of the cubicles gleefully
swatted his girlfriend. Men with exposed penises
walked around autistically entertaining themselves
with themselves. That night and every night it was a
club of the untouchables up for grabs. (Untouchables
in their own minds, that is, as many of them were
thoroughly attractive businesswomen, police officers,
and athletes. The spectacles in the rank closets were
mere shadows of the spectacles in the prosceniums of
their own heads. They were in denial of themselves.
They were fake zombies. I was the real thing. And

as their servant was the least and so the first, and so what?)

The weirdest thing about the club that I began to notice over the years was that time was a blur, as if it didn't entirely exist there. When I was young I used to drive my mother to distraction by asking her what time it was every five minutes. I lined ticking clocks on the table by my bedside, all set to the same hour and minute and second, except for those set to the corresponding hour and minute and second in other time zones, and all of those were correspondingly synchronized with each other. My bedroom was an echoing hall of all these tick tocks ticks tock. That obsession, though, was less an obsession with "being on time" myself than with the very foreignness of time from me. I was perplexed that something that seemed to be the very stuff of people's lives was so completely unfelt and unexperienced by me. I mean I had that sensation in countless areas. But time was where the shock of the difference hit hardest. Its reality was the furthest possible from how I felt and saw and was. "Does grass tick?" I remember asking my mom once.

Over the years, after I'd been abruptly weaned from my clock collection and banished to the garage by my dad, I'd grown more and more distant from time. When I came to live in the basement of the club Crypt, where there was not even the natural clock of the sundial of the sky to keep me aware of the passing of time, I had lost almost its memory and certainly any feeling of its impinging on my own time. What weirded me out even more, when I stepped back, was that my biological clock was similarly undone. Because my metabolism was so slow, my breathing so minimal, my pulse so nearly undetectable, my sweat rarely surfacing, I aged very little while the rest of those around me kept changing their appearance with lines and bags and saggings and furrows and crow's-feet and finally feebleness and paleness and white hair and fractured teeth. What didn't go wrong with their eyes and ears and hair and teeth and yellowing fingernails began to go wrong with their internal organs, their kidneys and hearts and livers and lungs and muscles. It was kind of sad. Although I didn't know which was sadder, the debilitating effects on those who were once ripe and were now prunish, or the loss I felt in myself as I was left waving to them as if from a dock on shore as they departed on the triumphant and cruel seas of Time and Death. By not really having a life, I was somehow Death's little friend.

I woke up to this experience of change on one particular night at the club. The kicker was the appearance of my mom and dad. I didn't even know that they were into the scene. But there they were. My dad now had gray hair flowing back over his skull. He seemed so much smaller. Was this the man whose threats had sent me fleeing further and further into myself? There with his brown plaid pants and white short-sleeved shirt, his tiny arms protruding from his truncated sleeves, wearing a pair of maroon shoes that might as well have been slippers, he cut an almost nonexistent figure. There was no scream left in him. My mother too was actually hunchbacked. Her disappointment had solidified into a stony face that bore the puzzlement of a thinking monkey's. She wore the fanciest dress she had, of this I was sure. But because she could no longer control her bowels, or the arthritis in her bones, or the pain in her varicose veins, she was forced to sit the entire time on a tubular chair next to a fake guillotine, her mug unwittingly reflected in visual echoes about eighteen times in a series of funhouse mirrors next to her profile.

I spoke to them briefly for old times' sake.

"Did you know I worked here?"

"We'd heard something," said my mom.

"No," said my dad, obviously a bit rattled by my peeking in on their dark, secret lives in the underground.

"We almost missed your shenanigans after you were gone," my mom said, causing me to bend down and kiss her hands softly for her sympathy and kindness.

"We rented out your old room for ninety dollars a month," my dad said, pleased with himself. "Thereby recouping half of our entire rent each calendar month."

"Bless you, but I have my routine of work to

carry on through," I said, shuffling off to separate a hinge of a cell door from a stuckness it had acquired from a buildup of oil during a slow week.

Mark was the next to appear. He was tall now. He had a mustache. He dressed in a black leather vest with blue jeans and boots. The usual. His chopped hair was brownish gray. His vest was marked with an insignia of wings and eagles made of raised red and brown leather. Very beautiful. He told me that he was a principal of a junior high school outside of Philly. He told me that if I came to visit him, I would have to clean his boxer shorts with my teeth. (I was glad he still had his sense of humor.) "You're still hungry, I can see it in those slits you call your eyes," he said, still capable of that nasty verve of his that had played more believably in the setting of our junior high school. Of course he had returned to the scene of the crime! Eternally recurring as the bully of junior high students, first as tragic little junior genius who could inspire groups and cliques to inflict pain on lone damaged lambs like myself, later as farcical captain of the ship who could induce injustice and misery by his power over single digits of salary in the pockets of workers dependent on such smallesse.

He told me to sniff his behind or he would put me in a sleep hold. I did for old times' sake. But I must admit to you, my weary readers, that I felt more pity than compelling salvation as I did so. Because, it was beginning to occur to me, Time is the true master, and we are all in his sway and are forced by our very molecules and genes to worship him, and no other certainly can compete. We worship Time and we fear Time, and that's the zombie truth. Zombies live longer because they are more obedient to Time. They don't try to beat it, certainly.

Sir Edward the M.D. by this time had long white hair. He was standing on top of a pillar in a far corner, beating the bejesus out of a lovely girl who was young enough to have been his granddaughter. While he did so he stuck all sorts of hoses and wires up his nose, in his veins, and then into her veins and nose so that they were knitted together as if by the snakes of a statue I'd seen in a book once, where snakes were all entwined about the body of a muscular middle-aged hero. When he saw me cleaning there he let out a hoot of a laugh. I hardly recognized him at first. "Zombie, you gotta portrait in the closet or something? You don't look a day over zero." I didn't understand his comment in the least, so I merely smiled.

Control Freak, the next to appear, had continued with his show over the years and certainly with the upkeep of his body. By now he was what he called a "one-strap guy." That is, he walked around in a pro wrestler's uniform (reminiscent of WSeal64735, whose loss I continued to mourn; if only he could have lived long enough to have seen the dark of the club Crypt, he would have been so pleased with me and it). He also sported the shoes with the laces that most of those behemoths wore. But he too was much older. The sinews he tried to decorate with extra fullness were incapable of supporting the extra pizzazz. His hair was depleted. Nevertheless he posed in the violent subterranean light. "I thought I sent you far away on a permanent vacation," he barked at me from the stage on which he was reenacting famous curls and squats from the historical past. He would know the names of their perpetrators. I was entirely lost.

"I did, sir," I managed to get in edgewise to his rotund curls. "And it was the gift that kept on giving. I found my roots. My identity. My bliss. And I've carried it with me into this perfect job of a life, where I serve others while serving Time with his carnivorous teeth. I help Time eat Life without anyone feeling any the worse for the wear. And I consider that the greatest service I could provide."

"Perhaps," he snarled dismissively.

I stepped off into the men's toilet room for a few minutes of respite. The man next to me was causing steam to rise up from his urinal as he peed into it. Even though I was the one who replenished the ice scattered at the bottom of the urinal bowl every evening repeatedly, I had gone for years without divining that the piss of these men was hot and so caused a steamy reaction when mixed with frozen water. Because of my own low metabolism, my own piss was quite cool to the touch. "May I feel yours?" I had asked one evening of a particularly spent individual. I was practically burned by his liquid fire. That's when I learned that lesson.

Finally there was Wendy, heart of my heart. She too was definitely showing the rings and circles and effects of the force of gravity called Time. She had gradually and almost imperceptibly become one of the schoolmarm women with her gray hair tied in a bun. Wearing a big black skirt, a white apron, and thick disciplinarian shoes, she had radically changed her manner, or at least her message, from the earlier days when her spunk was matched somehow to my own. As she served those drinks, I could always see near to her a big textbook she used when teaching her Woman class at a college in New Jersey, where she was now a tenured professor. Either because her eyes were failing her and she was too vain to buy glasses or because she was somehow less and less attuned to my condition of eternal lifelessness, she looked my way much less. It was as if she didn't see me.

But luckily that didn't interfere with her sense of duty, so that she never gave up on reading to me evening after evening before I turned into a caged breather and not much else. And it didn't interfere with my heart, which still burned whenever in proximity to her. Which I tried to be as often as possible. I would brush her hand with mine. I would tie my wrist with the bands of her apron that dangled behind her back. Conscious of her increasing difficulties, I would help hoist the bigger glasses to the top of the bar and clean up around her as much as possible. We were like the cartoons of the elephant and the mouse who lived in a funny symbiotic way, with the mouse cleaning the elephant's ears and the elephant clearing away obstacles for the mouse. The most interesting part of that cartoon, I thought, was that the two mis-sized creatures were actually held together by mutual fear, the mouse of the elephant's gigantic size, the elephant by his race's traditional skittishness. But between Wendy and me, for this first time in my incrementally maturing life, fear was not the program, or worship, but a kind of even Steven affection. It seemed to defy who I was. Was probably just a blip on my screen, perhaps even a glitch. Who knows?

That night Steve, with the black gray ponytail, big and burly, who was scheduled to have his thirtieth birthday party soon at the club, wanted his foot massaged. Very big: size fifteens. First I had to undo the buckle of his boot. All the while he was talking to his two blond lady friends. "Are you two gay?" he asked the one woman wearing a choker.

"We're in denial," she answered, as if she were telling a joke.

Next he wanted his back massaged. "Some bumps in my back don't go away," he explained when I pressed them.

All the while an auction was rolling at which a dollar was called a thousand dollars, and so on, I guess to add to the glamor. A woman who looked like the singer Deborah Harry set a record that night by going for "eight hundred thousand dollars." All through the bidding she'd spiritedly yell, "More," because she obviously didn't want the front contender for her hand to win. He did.

"I've got it, too. I've got it," he said when questioned skeptically by the emcee about the money, which he then flourished in stacks of bills he pulled out of a black doctor's valise like a gambler in the Wild West.

When all the characters finally left that evening, it was just Wendy and me reenacting the same routine we'd reenacted for what seemed like weeks and weeks and was probably more like years and decades. "Wendy, was it snowing tonight?" I asked.

"You've been asking that a lot recently," she answered. "I told you it's just that people are getting older and their hair is starting to turn white."

"Oh," I replied.

What I would do would be to put on my yellow cotton pajamas with the feet that allowed no skin to show anywhere beneath the neck. Then I would crawl into my cell and roll myself into a question mark. Wendy would seat herself in a corner, her black dress spread out like a pall, and read to me by the light of an industrial lamp hanging from a nearby corner. At her departure, which I never actually witnessed because by then I would be escaping into another kind of featureless world, she would extinguish the flaring white light. Then she would read to me from the play

Peter Pan, which was the only work of literature I really liked. On this particular night she reached again the last stage direction, for what must have been the one hundred and thirtieth time. "Oh, it was so lovely," I whimpered myself to sleep, the smell of extinguished cigarettes and spilt beers filling my boyish nostrils. The stage direction occurs right after Wendy, the real Wendy of the play, says to Peter Pan the line that Wendy used to say over and over to me during the stormy evenings of work to remind us that there was indeed going to be an end to the drudgery of other people's excitement. "Oh, Peter, how I wish I could take you up and squdge you!" the real Wendy said once, and my Wendy must have said a million times.

"This is it," Wendy whispered to me as she always did so that I mightn't be confused. And then she read straight out the part where Peter's Wendy comes back to visit him in Never-never Land but she is getting bigger, to his disappointment. He is becoming increasingly invisible to her, which she realizes when she says, '"Yes, I know." Peter's Wendy fears that he will soon find a younger little girl to be his mate in playland.

"In a sort of way he understands what she means by 'Yes, I know,' but in most sorts of ways he doesn't," Wendy read to me. "It has something to do with the riddle of his being. If he could get the hang of the thing, his cry might become 'To live would be an awfully big adventure!' but he can never quite get the hang of it, and so no one is as gay as he. With rapturous face he produces his pipes, and the Never birds and the fairies gather closer, till the roof of the little house is so thick with his admirers that some of them fall down the chimney. He plays on and on till we wake up."

I never heard her last words. By then I was always whimpering so hard that there was only softness left and the sense that I'd been coming from a strange place for a strange amount of time and that what was left was equally strange and therefore completely familiar.